1

It was Wednesday morning when an unseen hand added an envelope to the regular mail delivered to the old, renowned police station in the Warmoes Street, at the edge of the Red Light District, in Amsterdam. The envelope was addressed to Inspector DeKok. At first glance the content seemed ridiculous. Or was it? The note was short, laconic and lucid, written in an easy, fluid handwriting:

> *Dear Inspector DeKok:*
>
> *I have seriously decided to kill a man. For obvious reasons I cannot tell you the name of the intended victim, nor will I tell you the place and the time of the murder. In any case, that has already been decided. There are, however, just a few, unimportant details which I would like to discuss with you in advance. Would Wednesday night, eight o'clock exactly, be convenient for you?*
>
> *Yours very truly,*
>
> *[Pierre Brassel]*

DeKok seemed lost in the large, inhospitable detective room on the second floor of the station house, often described as the busiest police station in Western Europe. His tired and often painful feet rested on the desk. His short, strong fingers raked the gray hair that was usually covered by an old, decrepit little felt hat. His broad face, lined with the deep marks of a good natured boxer, looked solemn. He was not at all happy. He had read the strange note several times and every time he was again surprised.

This was new, entirely new. A person who contacted Homicide and detailed in a short, business-like letter his intention to kill someone had never before happened. He could not recall such an incident in his entire career of more than twenty years. This was something new and absurd.

Of course, there were plenty of instances when a murder had been announced in advance. But not this way. Usually such announcements were written in a flowery style, full of self-justification and pathos. And always anonymous. But this note, this short note, which wasted hardly a word, was signed. Signed with a real name.

DeKok had checked almost immediately after he received the note. He looked for and found Brassel in the phone book. He had dialed the number. By now he knew the number by heart. He remembered exactly the strange conversation that had followed.

"Hello."

"Yes."

"Mister Brassel?"

"Speaking."

"Inspector DeKok, Homicide. I ... eh, ..."

"Oh, yes. Homicide, Warmoes Street. Inspector DeKok, yes ... did you receive my note?"

"Yes ..., eh, ..."

"Fine ... is eight o'clock convenient?"

"Yes, that ... eh ..."

DEKOK AND THE DEAD HARLEQUIN

DeKok
and the
Dead Harlequin

by

BAANTJER

translated from the Dutch by H.G. Smittenaar

INTERCONTINENTAL PUBLISHING

ISBN 1 881164 04 7

Printing History:
   1st Dutch printing: 1974
   2nd Dutch printing: October, 1978
   3rd Dutch printing: December, 1979
   4th Dutch printing: January, 1982
   5th Dutch printing: November, 1984
   6th Dutch printing: May, 1986
   7th Dutch printing: October, 1988
   8th Dutch printing: August, 1990
   9th Dutch printing: April, 1991
   10th Dutch printing: May, 1991
   11th Dutch printing: August, 1991
   12th Dutch printing: September, 1992

   1st American edition: 1993

Cover Photo: Peter Coene
Typography: Monica S. Rozier
Manufactured by BookCrafters, Inc., Fredericksburg, VA

DeKok
and the
Dead Harlequin

"Fine, fine. Expect me. I shall be on time."

* * *

Before DeKok could ask a single question, Brassel had broken the connection. DeKok thought it inadvisable to call back at once. When he did call back, after about half an hour because he could not contain his curiosity, the line was engaged. It remained busy every time he called. Pierre Brassel seemed a busy man.

After a few more failed attempts, he had thrown the receiver angrily back on the hook. To help get his anger under control, he had stood in front of the small mirror over the water fountain and told himself a number of unflattering things for about two minutes, unflattering things about foolish people who time and again succeeded to plague him, DeKok, with near insoluble puzzles.

Finally he decided not to call anymore. He decided to just wait for the appointment. At least he knew that, somewhere in Amsterdam, there was a Pierre Brassel, who had written him a remarkable little note. DeKok stood up. With his typical, somewhat swaying gait, hands deep in his trouser pockets he paced along the deserted desks. He tried to form a picture of Pierre Brassel in his mind, a picture that would fit with the voice he had heard over the telephone. He did not succeed.

He stopped in front of the window, slowly bouncing up and down on the balls of his feet, and looked outside. His gaze passed over the twilit rooftops of the houses across the street and rested on the illuminated tower of the Old Church, so called because the "New Church" was a mere three hundred years old. It was seven thirty. He hoped that Vledder would finish soon, in any case before eight.

"And?"

With an amused smile on his handsome face, young Vledder looked at his mentor.

"Well, if . . . eh, you ask me," he said thoughtfully, "then . . . eh, somebody's is trying to play some sort of joke on you."

"A joke?"

"Yes."

DeKok slipped lazily into his chair and looked at the still boyish face of his congenial partner and pupil.

"If that's the case, my friend," he said with just a tiny hint of sarcasm, "when am I supposed to start laughing? At the time that the joker, Brassel in this case, lets me in on the joke, or when a murder really will have been committed? Tell me, please."

Vledder pulled a moody face. DeKok's remarks seemed to have offended him.

"But it's crazy," he exclaimed stubbornly, "totally foolish. I'm sorry, DeKok, but I can't see the seriousness of it." He snorted deprecatingly. "Come on, admit it, who would write such a note? Even if somebody planned to kill somebody or other, they're not going to announce it to the police. Nobody does that."

DeKok looked at him.

"Nobody?"

"Well, yes, somebody crazy."

DeKok rubbed his large nose with the back of his hand.

"So, you think he's crazy?"

"Who are you talking about?"

"Pierre Brassel is crazy?"

Vledder sighed deeply.

"No," he admitted, shaking his head, "no, I don't think he's crazy. That is, during my investigation today, there was no indication of that. On the contrary, the people I discussed him with, were almost unanimously agreed that Pierre Brassel is of above average intelligence."

DeKok nodded.

"That's too bad," he said hesitatingly, "But ... to be honest, I was afraid of that."

"Why?"

DeKok rubbed his chin with the other hand.

"Well, if Pierre Brassel had been known as a friendly, harmless madman, everything would be a lot easier. I'd just make one quick phone call to the guys in the white coats and we could take him into observation for a few days. But as things are now ..." He did not complete the sentence, but scratched the back of his neck. "What exactly does our friend do for a living?"

Vledder pulled a chair closer to the desk.

"Brassel and his aged father own a modest accounting firm along the Emperor's Canal. The business is highly regarded. You know what I mean, a left-over from the previous Century, an unshakable monument of solid respectability."

DeKok laughed.

"One calls that renowned."

Vledder made a nonchalant gesture.

"Have it your way," he grunted. "A renowned accountant's office, with a bookkeeper, a clerk and a darling of a secretary."

"Old?"

"Who?"

"The secretary."

"Oh! twenty three, chestnut hair, olive skin, green flashing eyes, an irresistible dimple in her left cheek, or, wait a moment, no, it was the right cheek, yes, the right cheek."

DeKok looked searchingly at his younger colleague.

"Apparently you spent some time with her?"

Vledder grinned broadly.

"Yes, in the assumed identity of an inspector of Historic Preservation, who came to look at the interior of the old canal house."

"Did you meet Brassel?"

Vledder shook his head.

"No, I managed to avoid that. When the secretary started to insist on introducing me, I quickly made my excuses and disappeared." He smiled at the memory. "It's a dank, old office, but the secretary . . ." He did not complete the sentence, but looked dreamily into the distance.

DeKok tapped a finger on the desk.

"What about family?"

"Who?" Vledder asked absent mindedly.

DeKok jumped up.

"Not the secretary's family," he said, irritated.

Vledder swallowed. DeKok's heated voice brought him back to reality. He took his note book from his pocket and read in a monotonous voice:

"Pete or, as he prefers to be called, Pierre Brassel is a handsome man, attractive to women. He's thirty three. According to my informants, he finished High School and College without any problems. He continued his studies and became a Certified Public Accountant, a CPA. Immediately upon obtaining his CPA he was offered a management position in the office. He's been married almost five years, has two children, a boy and a girl of three years and eighteen months, respectively. There's nothing known about friction in the household. The family lives in a nice villa, outside of town, just off the road to Schiphol Airport. There is almost no mortgage left on the house. The financial status of the family can be considered satisfactory."

DeKok grunted.

"Altogether a respectable citizen."

Vledder nodded.

"Exactly, a solid citizen. Not a murderer, or a latent killer. I've been unable to discover anything negative about the man. As far as is known, there are no skeletons in the closet. He's not known in the police files." He rose from his chair and began to pace up and down the detective room. He halted in front of DeKok's desk. "I don't know what *you* think about it," he said with a gesture of barely suppressed impatience, "but as far as I'm concerned we've already wasted far too much time on that idiotic note."

Thoughtfully DeKok chewed his lower lip.

"I hope," he said uncertainly, "I hope you're right. In any case, let's wait for Pierre Brassel. It's only three minutes until eight."

2

DeKok watched the clock like a hawk.

He noticed that the continued glances at the large clock on the wall became almost compulsive. He could not explain that. But his glance returned over and over again to the slowly moving second hand. It was impossible to resist the urge.

Driven by the same subconscious compulsion, he had checked the time an hour earlier with the telephone and he had synchronized his watch. For some reason he had the feeling that the time would be of vital importance; important to Pierre Brassel.

A few seconds before eight the sounds of footsteps could be heard in the corridor leading to the detective room and shortly afterward, an indistinct shadow could be seen against the frosted glass of the door.

Both inspectors looked on silently. Vledder annoyed and DeKok with tense expectation.

The arm of the shadow rose and knocked softly on the glass.

"Enter," called DeKok.

After a short hesitation the door opened and a tall, slender, handsome man entered. The first impression was confusing. There was something dualistic about his appearance, something like a Calvinistic church warden on a weekday. He wore a long, somber dark coat, but the pearly gray scarf which was worn outside the collar, gave him an elegant, almost worldly, appearance. The next most noticeable feature was the high forehead, accented by a receding hairline. A mocking grin seemed to play around the weak mouth with the thin lips.

"I have an appointment," he said, carefully enunciating every letter, "an appointment for eight o'clock exactly." He glanced at the electric clock on the wall. "I notice with pleasure that I am exactly on time. My name is ... Pierre Brassel." He announced himself like a TV-host announcing the next act.

DeKok looked at him searchingly for several seconds and tried to analyze his own, confused impression of the visitor. He was unable to do so. The confusion remained. Slowly he extended a hand.

"DeKok," he said vaguely, "DeKok with ... eh, kay-oh-kay." He pointed at his younger partner. "This is Inspector Vledder, my invaluable assistant."

Pierre Brassel grinned again and DeKok offered him a chair next to the desk.

The first skirmishes passed in a calm atmosphere. At first it was no more than a mutual, careful probing using platitudes and banalities, fleshed out with polite cliches. The first real emotions were elicited when young Vledder nonchalantly remarked that Homicide really could not be bothered with funny notes and that the police was not an institution charged with providing public entertainment. For that, he opined, there were different avenues.

The remark hit a sore point.

16

Pierre's eyes glistened dangerously. He spread his arms in a theatrical gesture.

"But gentlemen," he exclaimed, irritated and with a hint of astonishment, "surely you have not considered my note to be a tasteless joke? Really! The very idea is insufferable. In fact, it would be an insult to me, a very grave insult. I am not a charlatan."

Vledder grinned broadly.

"Oh, no," he asked mockingly, "*not* a charlatan?"

Agitated, Mr. Brassel stood up. Vledder's question had visibly upset him. His indignation did not seem like an act, it was real. A red flush colored his cheeks.

"But this is the limit," he cried angrily. "I did not come here to be made sport of. I wrote you about a case that, I assumed, would be of interest to your department. I want to discuss this case and you have agreed to this appointment. Everything according to common decency and politeness. There is no reason why you should . . ."

DeKok raised a hand in a restraining gesture.

"Please sit down and calm yourself, Mr. Brassel," he said soothingly. "I ask your indulgence and I apologize for my young colleague. But after all, it *does* seem strange that an intelligent man should contact Homicide in order to acquaint us with his intention to commit murder."

Brassel forced his lips into a winning smile.

"Your colleague," he said, much calmer, "is not just young and tactless, he also lacks imagination."

DeKok looked at him, his head cocked to one side.

"How's that?" he asked, interested.

Brassel sighed and resumed his seat.

"How can I best explain that," he said slowly, looking for words. "Well, for instance, if you intend to plant flowers, or shrubs, in your garden and you are not sure what is the

17

best time or method to do so, you will ask for advice from a florist, or a gardener. Logical, I should think. After all, they are professionals." He laughed pleasantly and gestured vaguely toward DeKok with a slender hand. "Well, I have taken it upon myself to commit murder and *where* do I go for professional help?" He looked smugly about, as if expecting a spontaneous answer from an attentive audience. Then he answered his own question: "Of course, from the famous Inspector DeKok, expert in Homicide."

There was a sudden silence.

DeKok looked intently at the gleaming, beaming face of Brassel and tried to detect a hint of facetiousness. There was none. He encountered a pair of cunning, alert eyes that carefully measured the reaction created by the earlier remarks. And there was a reaction.

Vledder looked at Brassel with, wide, surprised eyes and DeKok swallowed. It took a while before he trusted himself to speak again.

"I believe," he said heatedly, "that you have made a serious mistake. Your comparison is incorrect. Your premise is faulty. I'm not an expert in the committing of murders. I merely try to solve them, I mean, to find the perpetrators, afterward, when the murders have been committed *by others*. You understand?"

Pierre Brassel nodded emphatically and showed rows of white teeth.

"Exactly, yes," he cried enthusiastically, "exactly right! And that is exactly the *why* of my, to you, so ridiculous note. You have experience with murders. *Afterwards* you can say exactly what mistakes the killer has made and why should I not utilize your knowledge to avoid mistakes of my own?"

He moved his chair slightly and sighed deeply. Then he continued:

"See here, Inspector," he said earnestly, "you can only start your work after I have committed my deed. Not before, and that is too late for my purposes. I can not change the situation anymore, then. From that moment on, you and I have to be enemies. A normal, open exchange of ideas is no longer possible between us because, how shall I say it, because our goals are no longer the same. But right now, under the present circumstances, I mean, during the preliminaries, we could . . ."

He did not complete the sentence and seemed to weigh something in his mind.

"DeKok," he said after a considerable silence and with a more determined tone of voice, "I want to make you an honest offer. You tell me what mistakes to avoid when I commit my murder and I will deliver myself to you as the culprit."

Brassel smiled charmingly.

"Call it a gentlemen's agreement," he added.

He paused. When DeKok did not react, he continued: "In fact, you already have my part of the bargain in your hands. I have delivered myself to you. Only the murder is yet to be committed. You understand that is my motive: I want to commit the perfect crime."

DeKok rubbed his broad face with his hands. He peeked at Brassel from between his fingers. The visitor looked as if he had just spread the winning poker hand on the table.

"I do believe," answered DeKok quietly, "that I understand you. You expect from me, as expert in the field, a set of instructions for the perfect murder. A sort of recipe."

"Indeed."

"A complete recipe, including all the ingredients to guarantee you will not be caught, or punished."

Brassel nodded joyfully.

"Exactly!" he said.

DeKok pushed his lower lip forward.

"And in exchange I'll be allowed to know that you committed the murder." DeKok's voice dripped with sweet sarcasm. "That's what you mean, right?"

"Indeed, that *is* what I mean."

"It seems to me," grinned DeKok, "it seems to me a rather one-sided agreement. What good is it if I, as a policeman, *know* that you have committed a murder, when I will never be able to prove your guilt, because *you*, thanks to *my* recipe, have been able to commit the perfect crime. What's in it for me? Nothing! Absolutely nothing! I have a perpetrator, but will never be able to deliver him to Justice!"

Pierre Brassel gave him his most winning smile.

"You *are* clever, Inspector. You are right, I just want to escape the consequences." He shrugged his shoulders in a negligent gesture. "Understandable, do you not agree? I am still rather young, I have a darling wife and two wonderful children, a good position. It would be too silly to risk all that for a murder which is no more than a somewhat belated . . ." He halted suddenly and displayed a shy smile. For the first time it seemed as if he had lost part of his self-control.

DeKok looked at him, a challenge in his eyes.

"A belated what . . .?" he asked.

Brassel stroked his temples with the flat of his hands.

"You *will* find out," he said slowly. "Believe me, you will see. There is no reason to get ahead of the facts."

A new silence fell upon the room.

Vledder who leaned against a wall, diagonally behind Brassel, pointed at his head with a meaningful look. It did not escape DeKok. He released a deep sigh and directed his attention once again at Brassel.

"You are," he asked resignedly, "actually planning to commit murder?"

"Yes, I am. Even if you do not help me, do not give me the 'recipe'. I wrote it clearly enough, the time and the place have already been decided. Nothing can change that."

DeKok leaned forward and studied Brassel's face with care.

"Seriously," he said finally, "you really didn't expect for a moment that I would help you commit murder, now did you?"

Pierre Brassel looked up and shook his head. A sad smile marred his handsome face.

"No," he answered cheerlessly, "I did not believe that for an instant."

DeKok's eyebrows rippled slightly. There were those who swore that DeKok's eyebrows lived a life of their own. It was certain that his eyebrows could do gymnastics that were not within the capabilities of ordinary eyebrows. Vledder always watched with fascination. Sometimes, he thought, he could predict DeKok's actions, or words, from the way the eyebrows moved. But he was always wrong.

"Why did you write the note?" asked DeKok.

Brassel did not answer. He stretched his left arm slightly forward, pushed the sleeve of his coat back and looked intently at his watch.

"Why," repeated DeKok, irritated, "why did you write me the note?"

Brassel completely ignored the question. He kept staring at his watch, without raising his eyes. After a few seconds he stood up and looked first at DeKok, then at Vledder and then back again. His behavior resembled that of a toast master, about to begin the long-winded, well-rehearsed introduction of the next speaker.

"Gentlemen," he said in a solemn tone of voice, "in room twenty-one of the Greenland Arms Hotel, about three hundred yards from here, as the crow flies, you will find the corpse of Jan Brets."

"What!?"

Pierre Brassel grinned.

"Jan Brets," he continued cheerfully, "with a crushed skull."

He gestured toward the telephone on DeKok's desk.

"Please call them," he encouraged, "the Greenland Arms Hotel, or send one of your alert constables to check it out."

DeKok's eyes narrowed dangerously.

"Is this a joke?" he asked vehemently.

Brassel gave him a sad look.

"It seems," he said, shaking his head, "that you find it difficult to take me seriously. Am I right?"

DeKok bit his lower lip and stared at the strange man in front of him. He tried to penetrate the thoughts of his adversary but was again confronted by the fine line between joviality and seriousness on which Brassel seemed continually to balance. It confused him for just a moment, disturbed his equilibrium. But the hesitation did not last long.

"Vledder," he commanded, "call the Greenland Arms."

* * *

The three men stood grouped around the phone. Vledder dialed the number. The beeping of the touch tones was the only sound. DeKok's face was serious. Around Brassel's lips played a faint smile, a glow of triumph lit up his light gray eyes.

DeKok listened on an extension.

"Greenland Arms," said a voice, "Concierge speaking."

"Police," answered Vledder, "Vledder, Warmoes Street Station. Can you tell me the name of the guest in room twenty one?"

"One moment please ... yes ... that's Mr. Brets."

"Is he still alive?"

"What did you say!?"

"Is Brets still alive?"

A soft chuckle came over the line

"I handed him his key at eight o'clock."

"That was at eight o'clock. But is he still alive now?"

"I guess so."

Vledder sighed.

"If it's not to much to ask, would you please take a look in his room?"

"All right. Police you said? As you wish, please hold on."

Meanwhile DeKok looked at the clock in the detective room. It was a quarter to nine.

It took exactly four minutes until the concierge of the Greenland Arms manifested himself again at the other side of the line.

"Police ... police!"

His voice sounded scared, confused.

"Yes?"

"Mr. Brets ... Brets is dead."

3

Pierre Brassel stepped toward the door.

"I presume," he said with an elegant gesture of the hands, "that you gentlemen will have no time for me, at the moment. Regretful. Perhaps another time will be more convenient." He took hold of the doorknob. "In any case, gentlemen, I wish you every possible success with your investigations."

Vledder suddenly seemed to wake up from a daze. Impulsively he leaped at Brassel and took him by the arm.

"You're not leaving," he said, shaking his head, "no, you're not leaving just like that. No way! First you'll have to answer a few questions about this killing. Apparently you know a bit too much about it."

The tall, distinguished Brassel, so abruptly prevented from leaving, raised a cautioning finger.

"You do not have the right to manhandle me in such a manner." There was a barely concealed threat in his tone of voice. "You also do not have the right to keep me here. The concierge, and perhaps additional staff of the Greenland Arms, will be able to tell you that Jan Brets entered the hotel healthy and with an intact cranium. You will further be able to establish that he was handed his key shortly thereafter and that Jan Brets cheerfully disappeared in his room."

He grinned broadly, a little false.

"Further I beg to remind you gentlemen that I have been under your complete surveillance from exactly eight o'clock onward." He grinned again, mocking, challenging, with a twinkle of pure venomous pleasure in his eyes. "What more *could* you ask for. Nobody could wish for a better alibi in case of a murder."

Vledder let go of Brassel's arm, but placed himself in front of the door. He stood there, like an implacable Cerberus. His boyish face showed a grim, uncompromising expression. It did not seem that Pierre Brassel was going to leave without a struggle.

"How did you know," he barked, "that Jan Brets was going to be killed in the Greenland Arms tonight? Who exactly told you that? How did you know about it?"

Mr. Brassel gave a bored sigh in response.

"You are wasting your time," he said slowly. "I have already proved abundantly that I am *not* the murderer. What more can I tell you?" He grinned maliciously. "Or perhaps you would like me to tell you who killed Jan Brets?"

Vledder nodded, lips pressed together.

"Yes," he hissed from between his teeth, "exactly! That's what I want to know."

Brassel slowly shook his head. His handsome face showed utter contempt.

"But gentlemen," he exclaimed derisively, "where is your professional pride? I should expect that you would insist on finding the murderer of Jan Brets yourselves." His voice was sarcastic and the expression on his face was not pleasant. "Surely, the famous Inspector DeKok will know exactly how to proceed. Elementary, you agree? Find the mistakes that have been made."

He paused and looked demonstratively at his watch.

"I *am* terribly sorry. My time is limited. I have to leave."

He uttered a few more apologies and finally turned toward Vledder.

"If you would be so kind as to step aside, I could pass."

Vledder's face became red. He maintained his stance in front of the door and seemed little inclined to move. Sighing, DeKok rose from his chair. He came from behind his desk and walked over to Vledder.

"Come on, Dick," he commanded gently, "let the gentleman pass. You heard him, the gentleman's time is limited. He has to leave. We should not force our hospitality upon him." He smiled pleasantly, then added: "Not yet. Perhaps another time."

Grudgingly Vledder stepped aside, a look of hatred in his eyes. With a courtly bow, Brassel left the room. With an equally courtly bow, DeKok held the door for him.

* * *

Jan Brets looked grotesque.

He was supine with arms and legs stretched out wide. It was as if he had wanted to cover as much of the floor space as possible. That's how they found him, in a strange position with pulled up knees and bent elbows. In that position he most resembled a wooden harlequin, a marionette of which all strings had been pulled up tight. A life-size harlequin. It would not have surprised DeKok in the least if the arms and legs had suddenly started to move rhythmically, as if guided by an unseen puppeteer pulling the strings. The image of a harlequin was so all pervasive. The waxen, almost white face

27

of Jan Brets was frozen into a grinning, partly surprised grimace, as if he did not understand something, as if his own, sudden death was a huge joke of which he had just missed the punch line.

The complete picture was silly, ridiculous, but not macabre, or fearsome. Death presented itself mildly, without horror. A cursory examination did not even show any overt signs of violence. Just a small trickle of blood from the left ear, ending in an already coagulated puddle on the floor. That was all.

"That's exactly how I found him," repeated the concierge of the Greenland Arms in a voice still a bit shrill from excitement. "That was after your, if I may so, unusual phone call."

DeKok nodded.

"You may say so," he answered amiably. "I just hope you didn't touch anything."

The concierge shook his head vehemently.

"No, no, Inspector. I didn't touch a thing. Nothing. Well, of course, except the door. But that was hard to avoid. I had to do that. But I didn't go any farther than the door. First I knocked, several times. Only after I didn't get an answer, did I open the door."

"And?"

"That's when I found him."

"Dead?"

The concierge looked at DeKok with wide open, scared eyes. Hesitatingly he pointed at the floor.

"Exactly as he is now." His large adam's apple bobbed up and down and his fingers worried nervously with the buttons of his jacket. "He ... eh, he ... is really dead, isn't he?"

DeKok pursed his lips and nodded.

"He's dead now."

The concierge swallowed quickly.

"You mean, he was still alive, earlier?"

"You didn't touch the corpse, I mean, you didn't check if he was indeed dead? Did you feel his pulse, or check his breathing?"

"No."

DeKok smiled at the subdued face of the concierge. He placed a comforting hand on the man's shoulder.

"He couldn't have been saved, anyway," he said soothingly. "Please don't let it bother you, there was nothing you could have done." He gave the man an encouraging smile. "But now something else: was the room locked when you got here?"

"No." The concierge thought about it. "No, the door wasn't locked. I could just push it open."

"You have a pass-key?"

"Yes."

"Who else?"

"Almost everybody, except for dining room and kitchen personnel. Maid service and room service. Front desk personnel and myself. Of course, also management. Naturally, personnel is not allowed to use their pass-keys at will. There are very strict rules about that. First you knock, for instance. You know what I mean. You don't want to barge in on a guest unannounced."

DeKok nodded.

"How many pass-keys are available?"

"About twenty."

"And you know exactly who is entitled to have, and use, such a key?"

"But of course."

"Excellent," murmured DeKok, "really excellent." Then he continued, a bit louder: "In about half an hour I would like to talk to all who have such a key. Get them all together in the reading room." He pushed his hat a bit further back on his head. "For the time being you may leave us to it. Oh, yes, I would also like a list of all the guests, their rooms and a floor plan for this floor."

The concierge bowed.

"But of course," he said with professional servility. "But of course, I'll take care of it. I'll take care of it at once." Then he asked: "And can I be of service in any other way, gentlemen?"

DeKok grinned at the man and his obvious worry about the reputation of the hotel. The concierge was struck by the way it transformed the Inspector's face. A grinning DeKok was irresistible.

"In a moment," said DeKok, smiling, "two rather formidable gentlemen, dressed in dark coats and accompanied by large leather suitcases will arrive . . ."

"Yes . . .?"

"Please welcome them in my name and have them immediately conveyed to this room. Those two gentlemen, you see, are the world's greatest experts in the photographing of corpses and the taking of fingerprints."

"Oh," said the concierge.

"Yes," agreed DeKok. "And in case," he continued, "you spot any gentlemen of the press, you will be so kind as to deny them access past the porter's lodge. Understood?"

The concierge again bowed in acquiescence.

"Excellent," said DeKok, "really excellent." He closed the door of room 21 in the face of the bewildered concierge.

* * *

Vledder had been roaming the scene of the crime for some time by the time DeKok had finished his conversation with the concierge. He had inspected the bolts on the French doors to the balcony and was now busily engaged in a number of measurements to determine the exact position of the corpse. Meanwhile he worked on a sketch of the situation.

When DeKok turned away from the door, Vledder pointed at a hockey stick on the floor next to the door. It was an unusual kind of hockey stick. Apart from the handle, the blade, too, was heavily wrapped in tape. The tape around the blade was new, obviously applied rather recently.

DeKok took a clean handkerchief from a pocket and lifted the stick between thumb and index finger. It almost slipped from his fingers. The stick was unusually heavy.

"Goodness," he exclaimed, surprise in his voice, "this stick has been weighted. It seems as if something heavy, perhaps strips of lead, have been attached to the blade. It's hard to see at the moment, but I bet next year's salary that the bottom tape has no other purpose than to keep the weights in place."

He shook his head in astonishment.

"It has become a formidable weapon this way," he observed, "extremely well suited for the bashing of heads and such."

He looked at it closely.

"You know, young Vledder," he remarked after a while, "I think that this particular murder has been planned for some time. It's the result of a well conceived, detailed plan. Look at the hockey stick, for instance. The new tape has been very carefully applied. At first glance I'd say that it's the result of several hours work."

He sighed sadly.

"I'd say it has been worked on with a lot of care and devotion, better applied to more productive labor. The killer, whoever he, or she, may be, obviously took pride in the preparatory work."

Young Vledder did not react to the musings of his mentor. He did not seem interested. He behaved in a sulky way and there was an obstreperous look on his face. It did not escape DeKok. He replaced the stick where he had found it and walked over to Vledder.

"What's the matter, Dick?" he asked pleasantly. "Aren't you satisfied with the course of events?"

Vledder stood up, his measuring tape in the hand.

"No," he said, annoyed. "I'm not satisfied with the course of events. Not at all. I think you made a serious mistake."

DeKok made a helpless gesture.

"I'm really not aware of having made a mistake." It sounded like an apology. "Tell me, what mistake was that?"

"You shouldn't have let Pierre Brassel leave, just like that."

The old Inspector sighed deeply.

"So," he said resignedly, "*that's* what's bothering you. I thought so. I thought I noticed something like that, back at the office." He rubbed his broad face and then raised a cautioning finger. "Just take it from me, Dick, a policeman should always be extremely careful with intelligent people. They can cause a lot more trouble than the dumb ones. And Pierre Brassel is extremely intelligent, much more intelligent than you think. He's fully aware of what he's doing. And if we don't yet understand his motives, his background, that's *our* fault. That's a lack of insight on *our* part for which we have nobody to blame but ourselves, certainly not friend Brassel."

"That's not the issue," exclaimed Vledder sharply. "That's not the point! We should just have kept him and we should have interrogated him until he told us exactly what we wanted to know."

DeKok looked thoughtfully at his assistant, eyebrows rippling at a mile a minute. Despite himself Vledder was, as always, fascinated by the sight.

"I don't believe," said DeKok finally, hesitantly, "that we can force someone to tell us things he doesn't want to tell us. It's an ethical question with limits that every policeman must determine for himself." He paused. "But to be specific: please state the legal grounds on which we could have kept Brassel in custody."

"He knew about the murder."

DeKok nodded calmly.

"Certainly, that's obvious. What else?"

Vledder looked at him with amazement.

"What else? Even if we could not have charged him as an accomplice, he still had the legal obligation to warn the police, let's see, how exactly is that phrased? Oh yes, *at a time sufficient to prevent the commission of the crime.* He didn't do that. While he was acting the charlatan in the detective room and mouthing all sorts of nonsense, he calmly allowed the victim to be murdered in this room."

Young Vledder became more and more agitated. The blood rushed to his head. Nervous ticks developed on his cheeks.

"Dammit!" he cried, "he even knew how it was going to happen. Room twenty-one, the Greenland Arms. Jan Brets with cracked skull. He knew it so darn well, as if he had done it himself."

"And is that possible," asked DeKok seriously. "Could Pierre Brassel have killed Jan Brets?"

Vledder sighed.

"No," he admitted reluctantly, "that is, if the concierge spoke the truth and did indeed see Jan Brets still alive at eight o'clock."

DeKok nodded.

"Exactly," he said, "if we take that as our starting point, and possibly we'll find additional witnesses who can corroborate that, if Jan Brets was still alive at eight o'clock, then, no matter how much you regret it, then it's impossible for Pierre Brassel to have committed the murder."

DeKok looked around the room and then continued:

"I haven't seen any type of ingenious apparatus for remote control. The hockey stick was handled in an orthodox manner. I mean, someone lifted it with both hands and used it to knock down Brets. And that someone could *not* possibly have been Brassel."

He placed a fatherly hand on Vledder's shoulder.

"But apart from that, you're absolutely right. Brassel knew the murder was about to be committed. He did indeed have the legal requirement to inform someone: the police, or . . . the victim."

Vledder looked a question.

"What do you mean?"

"Well, exactly what I'm saying: the police, or the victim. The Law provides for either opportunity. Pierre Brassel is *not* guilty, if he warned the *victim*. In time, obviously."

Vledder made a wild, uncontrolled gesture.

"But, DeKok," he cried, irritated, "it must be obvious that he didn't warn the victim either. Otherwise this wouldn't have happened."

DeKok raised a restraining hand.

"Wait a moment. We have no proof of that. It's entirely possible that Jan Brets *was* warned, but that he simply ignored the warning. He could have considered it a joke. You remember how you reacted to Brassel's note? You too, thought about a joke."

He shook his head.

"No, friend Vledder," he sighed, "we can't do a thing about Brassel under the present circumstances. Any type of action would result in incarceration, we would have to lock him up, take away his freedom, and that's a terrible thing to do on such flimsy evidence."

4

DeKok pointed at the corpse on the floor.

"Well, Bram, what do you think of our harlequin?"

Bram Hessen, the rotund police photographer, forced his lips into a grin.

"Yes, well, a harlequin," he grinned again. "You're right, that's what it looks like, a doll with strings. In my opinion they placed him in that position on purpose. Let's face it, it's hardly a natural position."

DeKok chewed his lower lip.

"You ever seen this before?"

Bram shook his head.

"Never, I've never seen anything like it before. I've photographed a lot of corpses, but I've never found a corpse in this position. It's rather strange."

He walked carefully around the corpse.

"What was the cause of death?"

DeKok pointed at the hockey stick.

"It's almost certain that it was the murder weapon, a weighted hockey stick, probably with lead. It was used to bash his head in. Look at the blood from the left ear. It's almost certainly an indication of an injury to the base of the skull. But I haven't looked any closer. We're waiting for Dr.

Rusteloos. I expect he's on the way. Perhaps he can give us some clarification about the strange position. It really intrigues me."

Bram nodded.

"Yes, it's really weird. As I said, I've never seen it." He called to Kruger, the fingerprint expert. "Hey, Bert, you ever seen anything like it?"

Kruger shook his melancholy face somberly.

"No," he said sadly, "it's a new one on me, too."

Bram grimaced toward DeKok.

"And I've had to work with that for the last umpteen years." It sounded like a lament. With a sigh he unpacked his Hasselblad and started to make the usual shots, wide-angle pictures, details, close-ups. Bram used his camera with the hands of a master. He was an artist, accidentally strayed into the police.

Kruger was quickly finished with his search for prints and the dusting of same. The hotel room was not very big. After his virtuoso performance with the brush, the catch seemed minute.

Both experts were finished about twenty minutes later. They again donned their somber coats, hefted their heavy suitcases and disappeared—as they had arrived—with somber faces. Kruger did not even bother to say good bye. Bram turned at the door.

"If I were you, DeKok," he said, pointing at the corpse, "I'd look for a sinister joker."

"Where do you suggest?"

Bram pushed his lower lip forward.

"That's your business."

DeKok waved him away.

"Thanks for the hint."

* * *

Dr. Rusteloos wasted little time on greetings. He almost immediately lowered himself on one knee and started to explore the body with his sensitive fingers. When he turned the head of the victim slightly, the damage to the skull was clearly visible.

"It was quite a blow," he said, studying the edges of the wound, "As far as I can see, at the moment, it was but a single blow." He smiled bitterly. "But that one blow was more than enough."

DeKok showed him the hockey stick.

"Could this have been the weapon, doctor? The stick has been weighted at the bottom."

Dr. Rusteloos looked intently at the weapon.

"Yes," he said carefully, "that's possible. I can't give you a positive opinion at this time, you understand. I want to do a more careful examination of the body, but, at first glance, the stick could very well have been used as the weapon. Superficially I'd say that the wound could have been caused by such a device."

DeKok nodded thoughtfully.

"And doctor," he continued, "what about the position of the victim? The position of the arms and the legs. Is that normal? I mean, if somebody collapsed after a fatal blow on the head, is it reasonable to expect the body to assume that position?"

Slowly Dr. Rusteloos shook his head.

"No," he said hesitantly, "that's most unusual. I've never seen anything like it." He stared pensively at the corpse. "It's really strange, indeed, a strange position. It reminds me of something. It reminds me of . . ."

". . . a harlequin," completed DeKok.

"Exactly, right, yes indeed, a harlequin."
It sounded comical coming from him.

* * *

Further investigations in the hotel did not produce much.
The personnel had very little to say. All pass-keys were
accounted for and in the possession of the right people. No
key was missing. An elderly elevator operator corroborated
the concierge's statement. Mr. Brets had entered the hotel
at eight o'clock, at most five minutes later. He had picked
up his key at the desk and the elderly operator had conveyed
him to the third floor. He had even observed Brets walking
down the corridor to his room. By that time the doors had
closed and the elevator had again descended. Nobody had
entered the lift on Brets' floor. In any case, with the
exception of Mr. Brets, he had seen nobody else on the third
floor.

From the register they learned that Brets had arrived
three days earlier. He was registered as *Jan Johannes Brets,
age 25, merchant, 315 Brooklyn Street, Utrecht*. It was
assumed that the name was correct, because a passport had
been used for identification and the number of the passport
was listed. The accuracy thereof could be checked with a
single phone call.

Brets had checked in with almost no luggage. There was
a small carry-all which was found under the bed. The
contents of the bag *was* surprising. The bag contained an
extensive, well maintained selection of burglary tools.

From interrogations it was learned that Brets did not
mingle with the other guests. He did not associate with
anybody. As far as was known, he received no visitors in his
room. He only ate breakfast in the hotel. The rest of the day

he was usually absent. His behavior had not prompted management to consider him different from any other guest.

It was all very disheartening. The investigation in the Greenland Arms could be considered a dud. Once more DeKok addressed the concierge.

"Did anybody ask for Mr. Brets, around eight o'clock?"

"At the desk, or with the doorman?"

"Either."

The concierge was obviously trying to remember.

"No, not as far as I know."

"Telephone?"

The concierge's face cleared up.

"Yes, just a moment, somebody called."

"What time?"

"It must have been shortly after eight."

"Who called?"

The concierge shrugged his shoulders.

"That I don't know. The caller did not mention a name. It was a woman. She asked if Mr. Brets was in."

"And?"

"Well, I answered 'yes', because I had just seen him pick up the key. I asked if I should call him, or ring his room, but she answered 'never mind' and broke the connection."

DeKok nodded slowly.

"You have some experience with that sort of phone calls. Tell me, was it his mother, his wife, his fiancee, a lover?"

The concierge smiled.

"That's difficult to say," he sighed. "It seemed different from that. Not an intimate relationship like you mentioned. I would say more businesslike, cooler. She sounded a bit hurried, maybe nervous." He paused and was lost in thought. "There was something about the voice," he added after a while. "There was something about the voice," he repeated.

"What?"

The concierge pulled on his lower lip, roaming through the attic of his memory. Suddenly he looked up. "I've got it," he said happily. "I remember now. The voice had a German accent. You know what I mean, a German who's been living in Holland for years, speaks perfect Dutch, but yet you can hear . . ."

DeKok nodded.

"I understand."

The attendants from the Coroner's Office entered. They pushed the arms and legs of the harlequin in a straight line, shoved the body into a body bag, and placed it on the stretcher. DeKok watched their movements intently.

After the corpse had been removed, DeKok made a last round of the room. Then he locked the door and sealed it.

In the meantime Vledder checked to see how much time it would take to go from the entrance of the hotel to Room 21. It took exactly four minutes, including knocking on the door.

After more than three hours the Inspectors finally left the Greenland Arms.

It was quiet in the streets. Crossing the almost deserted Damrak, one of the wider streets in Amsterdam, leading to the Dam, the large square that used to be such a gathering place for Hippies in the sixties, they walked back to the station house. Vledder carried the hockey stick and the bag with burglar tools.

DeKok followed him. In his typical, somewhat waddling gait, he walked a few paces behind his young assistant. His old, decrepit felt hat was pushed to the back of his head. DeKok was thinking. Meanwhile he whistled a

Christmas Carol with sharply pursed lips. *Oh, come all ye faithful* . . . It sounded distinctly off key. He always whistled off key and always Christmas Carols, regardless of the time of year. In the center of the large square he suddenly halted. Involuntary thoughts drifted toward Christmas presents. Thoughts about the last Christmas. Then he walked on.

"No harlequin under the tree," he murmured.

5

DeKok nursed his tired feet.

With both legs on his desk, he leaned comfortably back in his chair and sucked a peppermint. He thought about the days when, under such circumstances, he would have taken a perverse delight in tipping the ash from his cigar on the freshly waxed floor of the detective room. But his smoking days were over. These days he only smoked for a purpose. Sometimes to annoy a suspect, or in an attempt to form a bond between himself and an overwrought witness. Sometimes he wondered if he did anything at all, that was not, somehow, primarily for effect.

The sudden demise of the merchant from Utrecht did not cause him any particular sorrow. He was not exactly upset about it. No matter how he searched his conscience, he was unable to discover a trace of pity, sorrow, or grief. But Jan Brets had been murdered and therefore he was professionally involved. In a civilized society it is simply not permitted to break the skull of one's fellow man. That was not allowed. The State had strict rules against it.

What really intrigued him, however, was the how and why of the deed. Murder was not committed at a whim, at least not yet. There had to be a purpose, a goal, a motive. But what?

From an inside pocket he took a wrinkled, official envelope and from that he pulled an equally wrinkled note. He handed it carefully to Vledder who sat across from him, slowly sipping from a cup of coffee.

"What is it?"

DeKok grinned.

"Found under the corpse of Brets. It became visible when they moved the corpse."

Vledder looked at the note with mounting amazement.

"But . . . but, it's been written by Brassel!"

DeKok nodded.

"Yes, a vaguely worded warning to the victim. But, I think, enough to keep him legally immune. Just read it."

Vledder read out loud:

"My dear Mr. Brets, I advise you not to enter your hotel room after eight o'clock on Wednesday night. Stay away. Otherwise a deadly surprise will await you. Signed: Pierre Brassel."

He returned the note to DeKok.

"And you found it under the corpse?"

"Yes."

"Not in one of his pockets?"

"No."

"Isn't that rather strange? If Brets had received that note in the normal way, I mean, if somebody had handed it to him, he would have put it in a pocket, don't you think?"

DeKok nodded thoughtfully.

"That would, indeed, be the most obvious thing to do. Therefore I suspect that Jan Brets never saw this so-called warning himself. I assume that it was placed with the corpse, *after* the murder, just so we would find it during our investigations ..."

".. and," completed Vledder, "at the same time would make it certain that Brassel could not be charged with concealing knowledge of a murder. Because, as you explained earlier, he had warned the victim."

DeKok nodded approvingly at his assistant.

"And that's the way it is, Dick. The makers of the plan have thought of everything. It's perfect, horribly perfect. I'm tempted to say almost flawless."

Vledder looked surprised.

"Almost?"

DeKok rubbed his hands through his bristly hair.

"They always make mistakes," he sighed, "always. There has *got* to be a mistake somewhere."

He made a lazy gesture.

"You see, if I were suddenly to believe in 'the perfect crime', I would at once resign from the force."

Vledder sat down at his desk and called Central Registry in Utrecht. The stream of information with which he was being supplied seemed unstoppable. He had difficulty making all the necessary notes. When he finally replaced the receiver, he sighed with relief.

"And what," asked DeKok, interested, "did our friends in Utrecht tell you about Jan Brets?"

Vledder grimaced.

"Well," he said with a broad grin on his face, "in Utrecht they don't seem very grieved about his death. I had the impression that tomorrow the Commissioner intends to treat the entire force to champagne."

DeKok laughed heartily.

"All that bad?"

Vledder consulted his notes.

47

"Yes," he answered seriously, "at least that bad. Over the years they have had a lot of trouble with Mr. Brets, there in Utrecht. Here is a sample of his crime sheet. In his relatively short life he's managed to break almost all of the Lord's Commandments. Theft, breaking and entering, robbery, everything, even murder."

DeKok grinned.

"Nice guy."

Vledder nodded.

"Indeed, you can say that again. As far as I can see, he's spent more time in jail than on the outside."

DeKok looked thoughtfully at nothing in particular.

"I don't quite understand that," he said, eyebrows rippling, "didn't you say that there was *murder* on his sheet?"

"Yes."

"What kind of murder?"

Vledder studied his notes again.

"Let's see. Yes, here it is. He was then just seventeen. During a week-end pass, *because of good behavior,* from the Youth Reform Institution in Haarlem, he and an eighteen year old partner from the same institution, broke into and entered a house. An old man, who resisted the illegal intrusion, was killed. The total loot from the robbery, according to the report, was less than ten dollars."

DeKok shook his head sadly.

"Terrible," he sighed, "just terrible. Less than ten dollars, the value of a man's life." He sighed again. "But this, this time he was not on parole, or anything?"

Vledder nodded.

"Oh, yes, he hadn't escaped, or something. When Jan Brets was killed he was free as a bird, just like you and me."

DeKok moved into a more comfortable position.

"But," he asked, slightly puzzled, "wasn't he punished for the murder?"

Vledder shrugged his shoulders.

"I readily assume that he was punished," he answered with a mocking tone of voice, "but in a manner that has lately become the norm in our friendly little country: with the utmost of humanity and understanding. He was still under age, you know. After the murder he's been arrested several more times, but has only gone to trial twice. Both times for a series of burglaries. He was only twenty two when he was caught after his release. So he probably got less than three years for the killing."

Lost in a sea of thought, DeKok stared out of the window for a long time.

"Ach," he said finally, in a somber voice, "What do you expect? Crime and punishment, vengeance, they're all old-fashioned concepts nowadays. These day it's more fashionable to feel pity for the criminal and we become more and more forgiving."

"You mean more and more criminal," Vledder said grimly. "These days crime seems almost a respectable hobby."

The young inspector snorted.

"*Sir*," he spoke suddenly in a strange, high-pitched voice, "*what do you do in your spare time?* Who, me? Well, I'm sort of a criminal. You know, every Saturday night a little breaking and entering, maybe hold up a gas station, just to calm down. Then, perhaps once a month a murder to relax completely, to get rid of the stress. *Well, doesn't the police do anything about that?* Of course, almost always. But you see, I have a number of phobias and other complexes. The psychiatrists and judges usually set me free immediately.

Don't even need bail. You see, I need the criminal escape in order to remain socially acceptable."

DeKok laughed

"Come, come," he said in a friendly, soothing manner, "come, Dick, don't be so cynical. It isn't quite *that* bad. You exaggerate. Anyway, the sentencing and punishing of criminals has nothing to do with us. As policemen it's none of our business. Happily so. Let's concentrate on Jan Brets and his untimely demise."

Vledder nodded sober agreement.

"You're right," he said resignedly "It's a waste of time to get upset about the judicial system. Also, perhaps I'm a bit prejudiced."

DeKok smiled.

"I once knew an old detective who would go crazy every time he had a case. His greatest desire was to put *everybody* behind bars so that the police could live quietly."

Amazed, Vledder looked at his mentor.

"Did he *mean* that?"

DeKok grinned.

"I think so, but I also think he was just very, very lazy."

The phone rang at that moment and Vledder lifted the receiver.

"For you," he said, after listening to the voice at the other end of the line, "it's the concierge from the Greenland Arms."

DeKok relieved him of the receiver.

"Yes?"

"There are two long-distance calls in the records for Mr. Brets," said the concierge. "Both calls were to Utrecht, to number 271228. Of course, we closed out the account for Mr. Brets and those charges showed up. The entire bill is of course a loss, or did you think that the family . . ."

DeKok ignored the remark. He was a master at ignoring things when he felt like it.

"Utrecht," he repeated, "two - seven - one - double two -eight."

"Does it help you?"

"That's difficult to say. In any case, many thanks."

He broke the connection.

"You heard the number, Dick?"

Vledder nodded.

DeKok began to pace up and down the large detective room. Something was bothering him. At his favorite spot in front of the window, he halted and looked toward the Corner Alley. His eyebrows vibrated dangerously and there were deep wrinkles in his forehead. There were a number of strange facets about the killing of Jan Brets. It was something new, something he had never before encountered in his long career. Again he reviewed the known facts.

"Jan Brets," he murmured to himself, "a character with, let's say, a certain notoriety, is murdered in his hotel room. The killer, who must have been waiting behind the door, attacked him from the rear and bashed in his skull. There was no evidence of a struggle. Brets was completely surprised. The murder weapon, the hockey stick, had been prepared some time in advance. Therefore, a well thought-out plan. This is confirmed by the strange notes from Brassel. The only thing which could possibly shed any light on it all, however, the motive, is a complete mystery."

He paused, sighed, then resumed his soliloquy.

"The only thing we know for sure about the victim, is that he specialized in burglaries during the last few years. We found the tools of his trade in the bedroom. Therefore, there's a reasonable presumption that the victim was in Amsterdam for some sort of burglary job."

Again he paused, rubbed his hands through his hair.

"But then," he said, louder and slowly, "the question remains if he was alone."

Vledder shrugged his shoulders.

"Possibly," he answered, just as slowly. "Or perhaps Brets was only here to reconnoiter the terrain and was waiting for his accomplices. Maybe he was just looking over the situation, so to speak."

DeKok nodded.

"Yes," he said thoughtfully, "that's a possibility. Jan Brets wasn't the type to do jobs on his own. His sheet seems to confirm that. He always had accomplices. Thus, there must be others who are aware of the plan."

"The plan for a break-in?"

"Exactly, Dick, the plan for a break, as you put it, a burglary, a robbery, somewhere in Amsterdam. A big job that required careful planning. Let's face it, Brets didn't leave his normal haunts, in Utrecht, to come to Amsterdam for something minor. Also the fact that a man like that takes a room in the Greenland Arms, a place which is certainly several levels above his normal choice for lodgings, must mean something."

Vledder stared at nothing in particular.

"You're right," he said slowly. "It had to be something special. And I wouldn't be at all surprised if his sudden death had something to do with it."

DeKok gestured.

"It seems a bit premature to come to that sort of conclusion. We really should wait until we a know a little more. For instance, if there *was* a plan, *what* was it? Who were the participants? But most of all, what induced Brets to come to Amsterdam? Was it a tip? If so, who was the tipster? Remember, Brets is an unknown in the Amsterdam underworld. I certainly never heard of him before."

Vledder shook his head.

"Me neither, although that doesn't mean as much. But what disturbs me: How does *Brassel* fit into all of that?"

DeKok sighed.

"Perhaps he's the brain behind it all, the designer of the plan. Who knows?"

Vledder looked searchingly at his older colleague.

"Then how do you explain the murder?"

DeKok did not answer. He stared outside. His face was expressionless. Suddenly he turned around and walked to the peg on the wall.

"Come on, Dick," he said, surrounding himself with his old raincoat, "I think we should make a trip to Utrecht."

Vledder's face expressed astonishment.

DeKok showed a serious face.

"It's never too late to console an old mother over the loss of her son."

6

Vledder and DeKok stood on the sidewalk of a long line of row houses in a dismal street in Utrecht. They had rung the bell several times and banged on the door for good measure. Finally an unkempt female head appeared at one of the windows. DeKok looked up in the gloom.

"Mrs. Brets?"

"Yes." The voice sounded quarrelsome.

"I'm sorry Ma'am," said DeKok in a friendly tone of voice, "I'm really sorry to wake you. But we need to talk to you."

"Now, in the middle of the night?"

"Yes, it's very important."

"I'm not at home for nobody," yelled the unkempt female head from above. "Nobody, you hear. If you don't go away, I'll call the police."

DeKok coughed.

"We ... eh, we *are* the police."

"Oh?"

"Yes."

"What you want?"

"It's about your son."

"About Jan?"

DeKok started to get a crick in his neck from staring up at the window.

"Yes," he yelled back, "about Jan!"

"What's the matter with him?"

DeKok sighed deeply. The loud conversation in the quiet street was not to his liking. Before long the whole neighborhood would be awake.

"Would you mind letting us in?" he asked, compellingly. "This is a bit difficult, like this."

"All right, then, just a mo."

The head disappeared.

A few minutes later they could hear stomping on the ground floor. A light appeared in the corridor and after a lot of rattling of chains and bolts, the door finally opened.

"Come in and don't look at the mess. I haven't had a chance to clean downstairs."

She shuffled away.

DeKok murmured something along the lines of: "Who cares?" and waddled after the woman into the house. Vledder followed.

She was skinny, raw-boned, with gray, thin hair that framed her face with stringy strands. A pale pink nightgown peeked from beneath a hastily donned raincoat. Thin, white legs emerged from beneath the raincoat and ended in old, formless slippers. The slippers were several sizes too large, causing her to slide, rather than walk. She led them to a small parlor where she sank down shivering on a stained sofa in front of a cold fireplace.

"Sit down," she invited with a grand gesture. "Put the dirty laundry on the floor somewhere. I should have washed today, but I didn't get to it. I'm not feeling at all well, the last few days. I may have something wrong with my back, arthritis, I think." She sighed deeply. "Ach," she added sadly, "when you get older, those things happen. The years will take their toll, you can't stop it. Old churches have dim windows."

DeKok nodded agreement. He pushed the pile of laundry aside and sat down next to her.

"My name is DeKok," he said amicably, "DeKok with ... eh, kay-oh-kay. This is my colleague, Vledder. We're police inspectors. We're from Amsterdam."

"Oh," she said, "from Amsterdam?"

She seemed used to police visits. It was a matter of supreme indifference to her. Only the fact that they came from Amsterdam seemed to arouse a vague curiosity.

"Amsterdam," she repeated, "Amsterdam."

DeKok nodded. Meanwhile he bit his lower lip nervously. He was still looking for words, had not formulated his thoughts properly. The old woman looked at him. In order to escape her questioning glance, he looked around at Vledder who leaned against the mantelpiece. The woman felt his hesitation.

"Well, what's up with Jan? Arrested?"

Her voice sounded shrill.

DeKok rubbed the back of his hand over his mouth. It was difficult to define the situation with Brets. He thought about it.

"No," he answered slowly, "he's not been arrested."

"What then?"

She scooted a little closer.

"It ... eh, it's something else. We found Jan in a hotel, earlier tonight. He ... eh, he's not well. Not well, at all, at all."

She looked at him with sharp eyes.

"What's the matter with him?"

DeKok swallowed.

"What's the matter with Jan," she asked, again in that quarrelsome voice. "You can tell me, you know. I don't get

57

shocked that easily. Not any more. I'm used to a few things, with him. What with one thing and another."

DeKok swallowed again.

"Jan ... eh, Jan is dead."

She did not visibly change. Her long, sinewy fingers reached for a pack of cigarettes and some matches on the round table in front of her.

"So," she said resignedly, "so, it finally happened." With shaking hands she lit the cigarette and inhaled deeply. "It finally happened," she repeated. He voice sounded strange, as if from a distance.

Slowly she let the smoke escape.

"It was to be expected," she murmured. "You know, it was to be expected. I'm not all that surprised, no, not surprised." She shook her head. "It had to happen, sooner or later." It sounded melancholy, almost wistful.

Vledder and DeKok listened to the rambling monologue. They allowed her to deal with the news in her own way. Silently they watched as she crushed the cigarette in the ashtray after a few puffs. Her movements were exaggeratedly careful. She kept crushing the cigarette long after it had been extinguished.

Slowly her attitude changed. The iron grip of her self-control relented slightly. At first the shocks seemed to come from deep within her. Unstoppable, like hiccups. Suddenly she clasped both hands in front of her eyes and started to sob. Her whole body now shook violently.

DeKok felt a deep pity. He placed an arm around her bony shoulders and pulled her softly toward him. She did not resist. She cried her sorrow, with long wails from an asthmatic chest. A poor, pitiful, much plagued woman, mother of a failed son.

It took a long time before she had calmed down. She picked up a dirty shirt from the floor and used it to wipe her tears.

"How?" she asked finally. "How did it happen? Or is that a secret?"

DeKok sighed.

"Of course it's not a secret."

"Well," she urged.

DeKok did not answer at once. He looked at her from the side and tried to estimate her resistance, her ability to absorb another shock.

"Jan was murdered."

"Murdered?"

"Yes."

She gave him a bitter smile.

"To tell you the truth, I thought the police had killed him."

DeKok's eyebrows rippled.

"Why the police?"

She shook her thin shoulders.

"It was the most obvious. It could have happened."

DeKok grinned, a bit embarrassed.

"I don't understand," he said.

"Ach," she said, suddenly irritated, "forget it! What does it matter now? He's dead. Why bother? What's past is past."

DeKok sighed. He seemed to do a lot of that, he reflected.

"Listen, Mother," he said seriously, "it's not a pleasant thing to do, but it's probably better if you know the facts. You'll hear them, sooner or later, anyway. Somebody, we don't know who, beat Jan on the head with a heavy object. It was murder. My colleague and I are in charge of the

59

investigation. It's not going to be easy to find Jan's killers. We don't have many clues and that's why we hoped you could help us."

The expression on her face changed. The mildness, the softness caused by sorrow, slowly disappeared. It was as if she suddenly realized who was speaking to her. Policemen! And not for the first time in her life, either. The memories of the past left a bitter taste in her mouth.

"Why," she asked suspiciously, "why should I help the police?"

"Because, . . . eh, because it's your civic duty," answered DeKok carefully.

She grinned, it was not a pleasant sight.

"My duty?" She pronounced it like an obscenity.

DeKok swallowed.

"Because it concerns your son," he amplified.

"And that brings him back?"

DeKok narrowed his eyes.

"No," he said, suddenly sharp. "No, that won't bring your son back. I'm not God. I can't make that sort of deal with you. I'd hoped, however, that your son's death would teach you something. But apparently I was mistaken."

He stood up and walked out of the room.

"Come on," he said to Vledder over his shoulder, "let's go. There's no sense in staying. We're wasting our time."

* * *

She hastily stood-up and shuffled after him. She overtook him in the corridor and grabbed the back of his coat.

"When is he coming home, sir?" It sounded pleading, almost scared. "Mister, when do I get my boy back home? He'll be buried from here, won't he?"

Slowly DeKok turned. Her words hurt him. He already regretted his sharp words, losing his temper. He looked down at her and met her gaze. A lump came in his throat that he was unable to dislodge. Her face again reflected the mildness, the tenderness, that can only be expressed by an old mother. DeKok had no defense against that. He placed his hand on the gray head.

"I'll take care of it myself," he said softly, "Jan will be buried from here."

A soft smile played over her face.

"Thank you," she said simply.

They took their leave.

Before the inspectors stepped into the street, she added: "Go see Fat Anton, he may be able to tell you something. He and Jan used to spend a lot of time together." She sighed. "Tell Anton I sent you," she added.

She closed the door and shuffled back to the room.

7

Fat Anton did honor to his name.

He was fat, rotund, big, with a triple chin and small, recessed pig's eyes above round cheeks.

He had not taken the trouble to rise. He received the inspectors while in bed. Next to his thigh, hidden by the blankets, was the indeterminate shape of a woman. Only the top of her hair was visible. Fat Anton scratched somewhere under his T-shirt.

"Well," he said, yawning. "Ma Brets sent you and Jan got banged on the head in Amsterdam."

"Indeed," answered DeKok laconically, "in a nutshell."

Anton looked confused.

"Well, just tell me," he asked challenging, "what's that got to do with *me*?"

DeKok shook his head.

"Nothing, absolutely nothing."

Anton's round face became more cheerful. He spread a pair of mighty arms and looked at DeKok with indignation.

"Well, then what do you want?"

Without waiting to be invited, DeKok sat down at the foot of the bed.

"Listen to me, Anton," he began amiably. "We have reasons to believe that Jan Brets did not stay at the Greenland Arms for fun, but that he was working on a job. And because the Greenland Arms is a rather chic hotel, we thought it might have been a chic job. In other words: a rich haul."

Fat Anton grinned.

"I like the way you think," he said admiringly.

DeKok rubbed his face with the flat of his hand and sighed deeply. He understood full well that he was not getting any further this way. He decided to change his tactics.

"Jan Brets," he said patiently, "was your best friend, right?"

Fat Anton nodded emphatically.

"Yessir, he was," he agreed.

"Excellent," said DeKok, "really excellent. Well, your best friend, Jan Brets, is dead, murdered. Somebody was nasty enough to break his skull."

"A dirty trick," reacted Anton spontaneously. "They shouldn't have done that."

DeKok swallowed.

"Yes, Anton," he said with a sob in his voice, "you're right, a dirty trick. And that's why I'm asking you, his best friend: is it possible that his murder has anything to do with the job, that rich haul?"

Anton thought deeply. It was visible. He rubbed a greasy hand over stubbly hair and a painful expression appeared on his face.

"It's possible," he said after a while. "It's possible, but I don't think so."

"Why not?"

"Nobody knew about the job."

DeKok sighed.

"But Anton, you knew about it." There was amazement in his voice and on his face.

"Well, yes, of course. I was part of it."

"Part of what?"

Fat Anton blinked his eyes several times in rapid succession and then laughed sheepishly.

"Well, you got me, eh? You got me. I have said too much already. Me and my big mouth."

DeKok ignored the remark.

"Go on," he said, "you were part of what?"

"Part of the gang." It sounded reluctant.

"What gang would that be?"

Fat Anton shrugged his colossal shoulders.

"Well, gang, you know, you could call it a gang, I suppose. It sounds sorta impressive. Real American, you know. But really, it was just a few of the guys."

"What guys?"

Anton shook his head.

"Gimme a break, Inspector," he said with irritation in his voice. "Jan and I belonged to a group. Alright already, so now you know. But you shouldn't ask any more. That's useless. I won't give you the other names, anyway."

DeKok smiled a winning smile.

"Excellent," he said, "really excellent. We won't discuss it anymore. You don't want to betray anybody and I understand that." He took a deep breath. "But something else: what sort of haul is it?"

Fat Anton looked reluctant.

"I'd rather not say."

DeKok looked at him evenly.

"What you mean," he said knowingly, "what you mean to say, is that now that Jan is dead, you and the others will finish the job." He made an expressive gesture. "I understand," he continued, "there will be a larger share for everybody else."

Suddenly a female head emerged from the blankets next to Anton. A young female head with black, curly hair and partially removed streaks of make-up on a pale face. Obviously she had heard the entire conversation from under the blankets.

"You," she announced decidedly, "you're no longer part of it. Not you. I don't care what the others do, that's their business. But you're out of it. To hell with the haul. I never trusted the whole set-up and now, see for yourself: Jan Brets is dead already. I told you from the start: I didn't trust that geezer. I didn't like him, . . ." Fat Anton tried to push the head back under the blankets. ". . that fine gentleman." she managed to add.

"Shut up, Marie," growled Anton, "it ain't none of your business."

"What fine gentleman?" asked DeKok, very much interested.

"Well," said Marie vehemently, "that geyser, of course, the guy who gave Brets the tip in the first place, that accountant."

"What!?" called DeKok, amazed.

"Yes, the accountant, come on, Anton, what was his name again?"

"Pierre Brassel?" asked DeKok hopefully.

Marie's pale face cleared up.

"That's it, exactly, Pierre Brassel."

* * *

With both hands folded behind his back, DeKok stood in front of the window of the detective room and looked outside. The early morning light already stole through the Corner Alley. The birds on the roof tops of Warmoes Street sang and chirped in a tone so clear and pure as if they were in a quiet monastery garden, instead of on the edge of one of the seamiest districts in Europe.

"What an evening, what a night," sighed DeKok, "one for the books. It's barely ten hours since Brassel walked in here and the mess began."

He bounced a few times up and down on the balls of his feet in an attempt to drive the lethargy out of his calves.

"A bit of luck that Inspector Meyden, in Utrecht, was able to tell us at once where we could find Fat Anton. I'm not all that familiar with the underworld in Utrecht. It might have taken us a long time to find him, otherwise."

Vledder came and stood next to him.

"But really," he said sadly, "we've not made any progress with the investigation. Fat Anton was not exactly a mine of information."

Smiling, DeKok shook his head.

"That Anton," he said, grinning at the recollection, "what a mountain of flesh. He almost needed the entire king-size bed by himself. What a colossus."

Vledder nodded.

"But it's too bad that, despite everything, he didn't want to tell us who else is involved. What target they were working on, maybe still are working on."

"Yes," agreed DeKok, "it's too bad. I would have given a week's salary to find out what sort of tip Brassel passed along. It must have been something the boys liked very much. To form any sort of gang, or even 'a group of guys', is not all that common in this country. The Dutch criminal is, by nature, a pure individualist. He doesn't form groups, at most he'll work with a single partner."

Vledder made a gesture.

"You know," he said, "when they have NATO exercises, the story is that the Dutch army is always rated lowest in all unit maneuvers, but the Dutch soldier is always rated first in guerilla warfare. Perhaps, with the inspired leadership of Pierre Brassel the so-called gang managed to overcome their natural aversion to cooperation. Who knows what he promised them."

DeKok looked at his watch.

"It's almost six o'clock. I propose we first get a few hours sleep. It's enough for one day. I asked the Utrecht police to send me the complete file on Jan Brets. They promised to deliver it to my house in the course of the morning. I'll read it this afternoon, at home. You never know. Maybe I'll find something."

Vledder looked searchingly at his mentor.

"And what about me?"

DeKok pushed his lower lip forward.

"Oh, I've something special for you. This afternoon I want you to go back to Utrecht and I'd like you to get in contact with Anton's Marie." He raised a cautioning finger. "Of course, without Anton being aware of it. I don't think she'll talk freely when her boyfriend is around. And I have an idea that the little brunette can tell us quite a bit about Mr. Brassel and his gang."

Vledder looked crestfallen.

"That won't be easy."

DeKok's eyebrows vibrated in that inimitable manner.

"Does it have to be easy?" he asked innocently.

"No, not really, but how will I get her alone. I've the impression that Anton guards her like a hen guards her chicks."

DeKok laughed.

"You come up with some crazy comparisons."

Vledder growled something unintelligible.

"Oh yes," called DeKok after him, "since you're in Utrecht anyway, call two–seven–one– double two–eight. A local number."

8

It was almost seven o'clock.

DeKok had been able to sleep until 1 PM. Then he had dressed and taken a short walk with his faithful dog, a boxer with a worried, wrinkled face, who considered his boss as his personal property whenever he was home. Some people said that the dog looked like DeKok and others said that DeKok looked like the dog. Either way, people were right. There was an amazing resemblance between dog and owner.

DeKok used the rest of the afternoon to read over the files on Jan Brets, forwarded from Utrecht. It had been an exhausting task. The behavior of Jan Brets had moved dozens of civil servants to compose stacks of prose. It was about six thirty when he had finally wrestled his way through the mountain of paperwork. And now he was back in the office, almost a full hour before his appointment with Vledder. He decided to take a little stroll through the neighborhood.

The neighborhood, in DeKok's mind, consisted of the famous, or infamous, depending on one's point of view, Red Light District of Old Amsterdam. The district encompassed a veritable labyrinth of narrow streets, small canals, quaint old bridges, dark alleys, unexpected squares and architectural wonders. All enlivened by exotic, often beautiful ladies, well-dressed pimps, innumerable bars and eating establishments of every kind. The endless streams of the sexually deprived, or those who thought they were and, of course, the bus loads of tourists from all over the world and the seamen from every nationality mixed with the locals of the centuries old quarter to create an atmosphere which could not be duplicated anywhere else in the world.

DeKok knew almost everybody in the Quarter, that is to say, almost everybody in the Quarter knew him. He was neither feared, nor notorious. He was simply accepted as just another facet, a different facet because he represented the Law, but another facet all the same, of the exquisite melange that offered so much pleasure, while hiding so much pain and sorrow.

But on the whole they liked him. The pimps and the whores treated him with respect. They knew he administered the law in a supple way, that he interpreted the dozens of regulations and guidelines with a certain latitude that was, although not in direct violation of the *spirit* of the law, perhaps to be considered as a unique vision on the *letter* of the law. And they were right. DeKok was unique. A buccaneer among policemen.

His old felt hat far back on the back of his head, the belt around his raincoat resembling a much twisted rope and a broad grin on his face, DeKok strolled along the old houses and the older canals. Here and there he nodded at old acquaintances, or familiar faces. They always smiled back, or greeted him cheerfully. A grinning DeKok was irresistible.

At the corner of the Barn Alley, he slipped, almost furtively, into the small bar of Little Lowee. Little Lowee, a small man with a narrow chest and a mousey face and owner of a bar frequented by pimps and prostitutes. Little Lowee considered himself a particular friend of Inspector DeKok.

It was still early and there were but a few customers in the bar. DeKok looked around. He spotted Annie, the girl of Cross-Eyed Bert. She had already drunk too much and DeKok estimated the intensity of the quarrel that would follow. He grinned to himself. It would probably end up with a fight. Those two lived like cat and dog for years. But neither seemed ever to be able to stay away from the other for more than a few days.

He ambled toward the bar and hoisted himself slowly onto a stool. It was his regular seat. From there he could overlook the entire room and his back was covered in case of unexpected eventualities.

Little Lowee approached with a wide smile on his face.

"How's crime?" he asked pleasantly. It was almost a stock question.

"Up three points," growled DeKok, as if he was quoting the Dow Jones. "It's a bullish market," he added.

Little Lowee laughed.

"Same recipe?"

Without waiting for the answer he grabbed under the counter and produced an excellent bottle of Napoleon Cognac, a bottle he reserved exclusively for DeKok.

After the usual ceremony—Lowee always drank a glass with him—DeKok leaned back against the wall and wondered idly why he had given up smoking. It had been more than twenty years, but at such moments he still longed for a good cigar while he listened to the piquant conversations between the little whores and the other habitues of Little Lowee's bar. It was amazing what they talked about when "off duty". Their "business" was seldom, if ever, a topic of conversation.

It was quiet right now. Only Annie provided a minimum of entertainment. Singing, she walked from one table to another. It was a sad song, maybe auto-biographical, in the meanest Amsterdam dialect. Loosely translated it was all about a naive girl who threw away her innocence and her virginity for a ten dollar bill. She sang it with a surprisingly good voice.

Little Lowee leaned confidentially over the bar.

"What about the stiff in the Greenland Arms," he whispered, "anything to do with you?"

DeKok took another sip from his drink and nodded imperceptibly. Lowee sometimes acted as an informer, but only for DeKok, and it was not necessary that anybody else ever found out about it.

"It were some guy from Utrecht, I heard. Some of the boys here knew 'im."

"Who?"

"Well, you know, some of them guys that hang around. I think they knew him from jail."

Grinning, DeKok nodded.

"Have you heard anything," he asked carefully, "about a big haul in the city. I mean, did you hear anything about plans in that direction?"

Lowee shook his small head.

"No, nothing, I ain't heard nothing."

DeKok looked at him for a long time. His eyes seemed to want to read the thoughts behind the small forehead. Lowee avoided his eyes.

"No?" asked DeKok.

A nervous tic developed on Little Lowee's cheek.

"Should I have?" he asked sullenly.

DeKok smiled.

"No, no, you don't have to. It's just a bit strange."

"Strange?"

DeKok sighed.

"Yes, Lowee, I can't help but wonder. If it was such a rich haul, why did they have to get a guy all the way from Utrecht. Don't we have professionals in Amsterdam?"

Lowee nodded emphatically.

"I should say so," he said, pride in his city evident in the tone of voice. "We don't need them guys from Utrecht for nothing." He picked up the bottle. "Another one, Mr. DeKok?"

DeKok nodded thoughtfully.

"Listen, Lowee," he said after a while, "If you go get a guy from Utrecht for a job in Amsterdam, what does that mean to you?"

Lowee pulled a face.

"It stinks."

DeKok emptied his second glass and slid off the bar stool.

"My dear Lowee," he said in parting, "you're right. It stinks."

And with that clarifying thought in his mind and two softly glowing cognacs in his stomach, DeKok left the small bar and walked back in the direction of the station house.

* * *

He stopped at the corner of Warmoes Street and looked at his watch. It was half past seven. He had plenty of time. But it was the time that tortured him. That was because he had no idea about what to do next. There was no rhyme, or reason, in the investigation concerning the murder of Jan Brets. He did not understand it. He did not know where to pick up the thread that would lead to the solution in the case of the dead harlequin. The harlequin was vital to the case. It was inconceivable that the killer had arranged the corpse in that particular position for no reason at all. It had to mean something. But what? He could not think of a single explanation that made sense. The entire murder was absurd. It seemed as if an insane person, an idiot, a fool, had figured out a practical joke, just for him DeKok. A practical joke so sinister, however, that he refused to believe that it was only a joke.

He pushed his old, decrepit felt hat a little further back on his head and looked around. About thirty yards away the blue lamp with the word "POLITIE" glowed in front of the police station. He did not feel like returning there already. Vledder would not have arrived yet, anyway.

Crowds of tourists shuffled past him. They came from the direction of the more respectable tourist attractions, such as the Rijks Museum with its magnificent collection of Rembrandts and now that it was getting dark, they converged on the Red Light District. Especially during the summer the old neighborhood seemed to be the main attraction of Europe. A babel of voices and languages engulfed him. DeKok looked pensively at the throngs. He suddenly remembered that Jan Brets, too, had spent three days in Amsterdam before he met his untimely end. What had he done during those three days? How had he passed the time? Who did he meet?

The questions chased each other in his mind. He waited a little longer and then, abruptly, he turned around and went looking for Handy Henkie.

* * *

Handy Henkie was an ex-burglar who, for no apparent reason, had suffered an attack of remorse. As a consequence of that, he had left the wide path of crime and followed, albeit reluctantly, the more narrow path of respectability. He slipped but seldom. Henkie had always considered DeKok to be the greatest influence in his "redemption". As a token of thanks and appreciation and to remove temptation from his path, Henkie had presented DeKok with his complete instrumentarium. It was an assortment of strange tools and specialized hybrids of more normal tools, usually of Henkie's own invention because he was also a gifted tool-and-die maker. Most of the instruments required long sessions of practice before DeKok was familiar with them. Sometimes, when absolutely necessary, DeKok would utilize Henkie's tools and talents when he absolutely, positively had to get in somewhere. Henkie had never failed him.

* * *

DeKok breathed deeply. Laboriously he hoisted his two hundred pounds up the narrow, creaking stairs. He hoped that Henkie would be home. The mere idea that he might have climbed to the fourth floor on a fool's errand, affected his mood. He was already asking himself if he had not been too impulsive. Perhaps he should have asked Henkie to come to the office.

When his breathing was more or less under control, he knocked and entered simultaneously. Henkie, slippers on his feet, was watching television. His mouth opened in surprise when he recognized his visitor. A tic developed along his jaw. He seemed struck speechless.

77

DeKok walked over to the TV and calmly pulled the plug out of the wall socket. The image of a talking man faded into a black screen. The echo of the voice remained momentarily in the room.

The Inspector smiled pleasantly at Henkie.

"I hate TV when I come calling," he said. He paused, then continued: "It's so distracting. By the way, good evening."

Henkie swallowed.

"Good evening, Inspector."

DeKok nodded encouragingly.

"Good evening, Henkie."

He lowered himself in an easy chair, placed his old hat on the floor next to him, unbuttoned the top buttons of his raincoat and stretched his legs comfortably in front of him. Meanwhile he looked at Handy Henkie who nervously pulled on his shirt. DeKok enjoyed the confusion of his host.

"I suddenly felt the need to pay you a visit," he started cheerily. "I haven't seen you for some time and I wondered . . ."

"You wondered what?"

There was suspicion in Henkie's voice.

DeKok made a gesture.

" . . . I wondered how you were. You see, that's what I wondered about. I was just concerned."

Henkie laughed. It was a strange, nervous laugh. At the same time his sharp eyes alertly explored DeKok's face. He knew that face. It had become familiar over the years, from many conversations and even more interrogations. The deep wrinkles in the forehead, the bushy eyebrows with a life of their own, the friendly, gray eyes, it was all there. Even the half-amused lines around the mouth from which one never knew if it said what was meant.

"I'm all right."

DeKok grinned.

"I can see that, I can see that. You're in better shape than Jan Brets."

It hit a nerve. Henkie reacted vehemently.

"That's a rotten thing to say," he cried out. "A stinking, rotten thing to say. Jan Brets is dead. I done read it in the paper."

DeKok nodded slowly.

"Yes," he admitted with a sigh, "Brets is dead. Somebody bashed him on the head."

Henkie moved in his chair.

"So, what's it to me?"

"That's one of the things I wonder about."

Henkie grinned without mirth.

"That's what you came here for?"

"Yes."

"You means it?"

"I mean it."

Suddenly Henkie rose from his chair, he gestured wildly, like a pitchman trying to sell snake oil. There was a hint of fear in his eyes.

"But, DeKok," he yelled desperately, "you *knows* me! You knows how I is, DeKok. I ain't got no truck with murder! I ain't that way . . . I can't even kill no fly, let alone a person." He almost stuttered with misery.

DeKok looked at him unemotionally.

"Sit down," he commanded. "Did I say that you had committed murder?"

"Geez, you scared me," Henkie answered, licking his dry lips. "Murder, as if it ain't nothing."

DeKok leaned slightly forward.

"Did you know Brets?"

"Yes."

"How?"

"From stir. A few years ago, when I was in stir in Haarlem, I met 'im. He usta walk with me in the yard. He was a kracker, you knows, armed robbery, burglary with violence. Filthy son-of-a-bitch, iffen you ask me. Ready for anything."

"Even murder?"

Henkie nodded assent.

"Yep, that's what I says. One of them guys that would do anything. You knows, no morals, anti, anti . . . something or other."

"Anti-social," supplied DeKok without thinking. He rubbed the back of his hand over his face. Then he asked:

"What did he want from you?"

"From me?"

"Yes."

"Nix."

DeKok's eyebrows seemed to reach his hairline. With a slight ripple they subsided again.

"But he was here, this week."

Henkie's eyes narrowed. He thought at top speed. Wondered whether DeKok knew, or was guessing. It could be a bluff.

"What, here?" he said finally.

"Yes."

Again Henkie flicked his tongue along his dry lips.

"Jan Brets ain't been here."

DeKok sighed demonstratively.

"Listen to me, Henkie," he said pleasantly, patiently. "You know I have a weak spot for you, but if I were you I wouldn't count too much on that, under the circumstances. Look, when we found Brets in the hotel room we also found a bag of tools and there were items in that bag that could only have been figured out by your, rather . . . eh, unique talent. That's how we know you must have seen him, you understand?"

Henkie bowed his head.

"Dammit," he said sadly, "you ain't never gonna leave me alone."

DeKok grinned.

"So, he *was* here?"

"Yes."

"What for?"

Henkie stared in front of him and did not answer. There was a melancholy look on his face.

"I didn't go back, you know," he said after a long pause. "Maybe you think I did?" It sounded glum. "I just made some stuff for him, a few tools, is all, that ain't against the law, is it?"

"Burglary tools?"

Henkie made a wild gesture.

"Wadda you want from me? It ain't against the law. You could close all the hardware stores tomorrow, if it were that. You can get a crowbar anywheres."

DeKok laughed.

"Did Brets just come for the tools?"

"No, he wanted me in."

"In what?"

Henkie grimaced.

"Something big, an . . . eh, an orga . . . an organization, a gang. You knows, like them gangsters in the States, or the Limeys. A brain at the top, who figures all the angles."

"So?"

"Oh, yes. They coulda used me, he said." Henkie made a nonchalant gesture. "You knows, me experience, me know-how and things."

DeKok nodded.

"And?"

"What and?"

"Did you join?"

Henkie's face was a picture of indignation.

"Didn't I promise you, then?" he answered, offended to the deepest part of his so recently reformed soul. "I did promise you I'd quit, didn't I? I just don't feel like it no more. I've gotta good job, now. Regular pay." He pointed around the room. "Just lookit, nice furniture, a TV, good stuff and all legit. I never made that much with me breakies and iffen I did, I'd be too scared to spend it."

DeKok laughed.

"So, Jan Brets talked about an organization. Did he tell you anything else, for instance, who was the leader. I assume that Brets trusted you?"

Handy Henkie nodded emphatically.

"Oh, sure he did. He trusted me. Didn't he ask me to join up, then? Now, that mean he trusted me, don't it? The boss, he said, was a constant."

"An accountant," corrected DeKok.

"Yeah, right, an accountant. You know, one of them geezers that looks after the cash for them big companies. Well, go figure, a guy like that knows where the big loot is. The boys only had to go and pick it up." He pursed his lips and his eyes sparkled. "It sounded real good, yessir, it did. It sounded real good."

DeKok looked at him searchingly.

"But Jan Brets is dead," he said callously. "It couldn't have been all that good."

Henkie nodded a bit vaguely.

"Jan Brets is dead," he repeated somberly. He made the sign of the cross. "God rest his soul."

They remained silent.

"Had something happened already?" asked DeKok. "I mean, had they already finished the job?"

Henkie shook his head.

"Nah, the thing were still in the planning, so to speak. But it was to happen soon, he said."

"When?" asked DeKok greedily. "And where?"

Again Henkie shook his head.

"He didn't say."

"Why not?"

"Geez, that ain't all that hard to figure out. After all, I'm an old hand at this sorta thing. Suppose I was to go after it meself. The loot woulda been gone by the time they got around to it."

He grinned at the thought.

DeKok rubbed his hand along his chin.

"But," he tried, "Jan Brets must have told you something about the job? After all, he tried to get you to join them."

Henkie shrugged his shoulders in supreme indifference.

"Not how, or where, if that's what you mean. They had a name for it. A code name, you know."

"A code name?"

Henkie nodded.

"Operation Harlequin."

"What!?"

"Operation Harlequin. Crazy name ain't it?"

DeKok swallowed.

9

Much to his surprise, DeKok found his old Commissaris (a rank equivalent to Captain) waiting for him in the detective room. The old man seldom interfered with his cases. Therefore DeKok found it difficult to suppress an expression of amazement, when he found his old boss in the company of Vledder. Both were sitting on chairs in front of his desk.

"Good evening, Commissaris."

The distinguished police chief rose from his chair.

"Good evening, DeKok. Vledder told me that you would be here at eight." He looked at his watch. "It's almost nine, now. Anyway, since I was around, I wanted to talk to you about the Brets case. Of course, I've read your preliminary reports, but they were a little too summarized for my liking. I would like more particulars. The press won't leave me alone. Apparently they got wind that the murder was discovered to have been committed in, let's say, unusual circumstances. And now they're coming up with the wildest theories. I think that the concierge of the Greenland Arms may have said too much."

He turned completely toward DeKok.

"Further, I'm curious to hear your plans in regard to Pierre Brassel. What are you going to do about him?"

"Nothing."

The Commissaris looked at him as if he was thunderstruck.

"Nothing?"

"That's right."

"But DeKok," exclaimed the Commissaris, apparently completely confused, "that man, Pierre Brassel, maintains, or maintained, more or less regular contact with the killer. Surely, that's obvious."

Slowly DeKok divested himself of his hat and raincoat. He did not feel like discussing the case with the Commissaris. It made no sense and it only complicated matters. He would much rather go his own way. But as a good subordinate he had certain duties.

"It may be obvious," he repeated slowly, "but as far as I know, it's not against the law to merely know a killer."

The Commissaris sighed.

"That's not the issue," he said, slightly irritated, "what I mean is that, via Brassel, you can find the real killer. I just discussed it with Vledder and I understand you let Brassel go, just like that." The Commissaris snapped his fingers.

DeKok shrugged his shoulders.

"What should I have done?"

"D-done, done!?" stuttered the Commissaris, "You should have had him followed."

DeKok grinned. Vledder watched carefully. Not even the Commissaris seemed immune to that irresistible grin.

"It would have been a waste of time and personnel. Pierre Brassel isn't crazy, although his letter might lead one to believe otherwise. The entire plan has been devised to keep the actual killer out of harm's way. Brassel voluntarily acts as a red herring. His only aim is to draw attention. It's no more than a feint. One does not have to be clairvoyant to see that."

The Commissaris swallowed.

"The last was not a nice remark, DeKok," he said sternly.

DeKok bent his head in shame.

"Sorry, sir," he answered quickly, "I really didn't mean it sarcastically. I just wanted to make clear that shadowing Pierre Brassel is likely to be unproductive."

Again the Commissaris sighed deeply.

"Alright," he said resignedly, "alright, already. I leave things to you, shall I? In any case I would like an extensive report on my desk tomorrow. You know how persistent the press can be and I would like to know how much, if anything, I can tell them. I certainly don't want your investigations hampered by premature speculations in the press."

"Thank you," said DeKok.

The Commissaris greeted them urbanely and left the detective room. The Commissaris was a gentleman, and would always be a gentleman, even when confronted with stubborn, or unwilling personnel. Vledder sighed when he had left.

"I really couldn't help it," he said apologetically, "really, it wasn't my fault. When I got here at eight, I met the Commissaris in the corridor. I had to follow him to his office, at once. He kept asking all sorts of questions and was terribly interested in Pierre Brassel."

DeKok nodded.

"Most understandable," he said. "After all, it *is* a strange business and he *is* the chief. He has every right to know everything."

He paused.

"Now for something completely different: What happened in Utrecht?"

Young Vledder shook his head sadly.

"I don't think," he said, dispirited, "that my trip was an unqualified success."

Amused, DeKok looked down on him.

"No success at all?"

"I followed Fat Anton and his Marie for hours. It was torture. He never left her side for a moment. Happily Fat Anton isn't all that smart, or he would have noticed me several times." Thoughtfully he stared at nothing at all. Then he continued: "Strangely enough, Marie spotted me almost at once. But she didn't say a thing to Anton. That's to say, I didn't notice that she did. You see, that's why I finally decided to pass her a note."

DeKok's eyebrows rippled briefly.

"A note?"

"Yes, in some bar. Anton had gone to the men's room. I wrote a quick note, asking her to come here tonight, without Anton, obviously. I managed to slip it to her before Anton returned."

Vledder made a helpless gesture.

"I know it's a gamble. If she shows it to Anton, it's all over. But I didn't know what else to do and I had to contact her somehow."

DeKok nodded encouragingly.

"Under the circumstances it was the best you could do, probably the only thing you could do. We'll just have to wait. Possess your soul in patience, my boy."

"What!?"

DeKok smiled.

"Possess your soul in patience. My mother used to say that when there wasn't a thing you could do about something. She meant you just had to wait. A saying, that's all. A bit old fashioned, maybe, but nevertheless true." He scratched behind his ear. "What about the phone number?"

"Nothing, no answer. I tried several times."

DeKok nodded.

"We'll figure it out tomorrow. Utrecht information should be able to tell us who belongs to that number. Maybe we can approach it from that angle. Who knows . . ."

The phone rang at that moment.

"This is the desk," said the voice of Corporal Bisterman. "A Marie Sailmaker for you."

"Is she alone?"

"Yes."

DeKok winked at Vledder.

"Excellent, really excellent. Please have Marie come up."

* * *

After a soft knock on the door, Marie entered the detective room with decisive steps. Her steps were a bit too firm and decisive for her elegant, high heeled evening shoes; just a little inelegant which created a comic effect. She approached DeKok purposefully.

"You wanted me?"

She was not quite as small as she had seemed next to the enormous thighs of Fat Anton. She had a very attractive figure and she knew it. Her beige coat closed tightly around a slim figure. A large fur collar covered the bottom half of her face. Her breathing was visible by the movement of the hair in the long fur; like a soft wind over a corn field. She took off a glove and placed Vledder's wrinkled note on the desk.

"Well," she challenged, "here I am."

DeKok gave her one of his sweetest smiles.

"My name is DeKok," he said pleasantly, "DeKok with kay-oh-kay. This is my invaluable colleague, Vledder. I don't remember having been introduced to you last night." Still smiling, he offered his hand.

She shook it in a businesslike fashion.

"I'm Marie Sailmaker."

"How young?"

She chirped like a schoolgirl.

"Guess."

"Twenty," lied DeKok.

She made a movement as if to pirouette.

"You can add five to that."

DeKok forced his face into an expression whereby amazement and admiration seemed to battle for supremacy. He pointed at the chair next to his desk.

"Please sit down," he said with old-world charm and a slight bow. "We wanted to have a serious conversation with you and therefore we used this, . . . eh, unorthodox method of contacting you. Do forgive me." He seated himself behind the desk and continued: "You see, my colleague and I both had the impression, last night, that you are an intelligent young woman and you would probably be upset if your friend Anton were to get into difficulties, or perhaps worse. It isn't at all impossible that Anton, too, will be . . ." He did not complete the sentence, but gauged her reaction.

Marie opened the collar of her coat a little. Her sparkling green eyes explored the face of the old inspector. She weighed the value of his words. She was not so sure of herself, now. There was a battle going on within her. She obviously had trouble reconciling her natural aversion against and suspicion of the police with the need to do something for Anton. She decided she could trust the friendly, almost fatherly face of the man behind the desk. DeKok noticed the inner turmoil with interest.

"Does Anton know you're here?"

"No."

"You didn't show him the note?"

"No."

"Why not?"

She did not answer at once. She changed position in the chair and pulled her skirt lower over her knees.

"Anton is an ass."

"An ass?" asked DeKok.

"Yes, an ass," she repeated sharply. "A big, fat stupid ass. Don't ask me how come I love that mountain of flesh, but I do." She paused. "You want to make something out of that?"

Slowly DeKok shook his head.

"Everybody," he said earnestly, "is entitled to love."

She nodded agreement.

"Exactly, that's how it is. Believe me, there is a good heart in that boy. He's a bit naive." She smiled tenderly. "A big, naive, good hearted man. That's him. There's no malice in him."

Her face took on a happy glow.

"He's a darling, almost a child, still."

DeKok sighed.

"If we keep this up," he said dryly, "I'll be wondering how that little cherub of yours got lost here on earth with us common mortals."

She looked confused.

"What!?"

DeKok grinned.

"I mean, let's not exaggerate. Your Anton isn't that much of a dear. After all he was, or still is, a gang member. Believe me, that was not because of any humane impulses."

Her green eyes spat fire.

"That's because of Jan Brets, the bastard. He made my Anton crazy. Brets with all his stories about big hauls, lots of money and no risks. Poor Anton would swallow it all, listen with glowing ears. You see, Anton can't think for himself. He's always happy to let someone else do the thinking for him. Well, Jan Brets was one of those who thought for him and . . ."

She pressed her lips together. She paused a long time before she continued.

"Jan Brets with all his jokes and big plans, he's dead. Somebody was faster than me, believe me, otherwise I would have fed him some rat poison, one of these days." She rummaged in her purse and took out a cigarette. She lit up. Her hands shook. She blew smoke toward the ceiling.

"Of course, it's stupid," she said in an even voice, "to say something like that to the police, but I would like you to know how I thought about Jan Brets."

DeKok nodded.

"It's very clear to me," he said laconically. He looked at her and then asked: "When did you first hear about the accountant?"

Pensively she chewed her lower lip. In an indefinable way, it made her look more attractive. Some of the hardness had left her face.

"About two weeks ago. That's when he mentioned his name, Pierre Brassel. Usually he referred to him as his little gold mine."

"Gold mine?"

She nodded, crushed out her cigarette.

"Yes, Jan Brets meant the accountant with that. Look," she explained, "an accountant deals with a lot of big businesses. He knows exactly how much cash they have, where they keep it, how it is protected, everything. He was going to tip off Jan Brets and Jan and a bunch of guys, including my Anton, would go in and clean up."

"A nice plan."

"Yessir, and that's why my Anton was so keen on it." DeKok nodded.

"How many times did you meet Brassel?"

Thinking, she placed a long finger alongside her nose.

"Just once. About a week ago. In the evening. Brets brought him to Anton's house. For discussions." She snorted derisively.

"And you were there?"

"Yes."

"You know what was discussed?"

"Yes."

Slowly DeKok rose from his chair and started to pace up and down the room. He wanted to give her time to realize what she was doing. Experience had taught him that it was counter-productive to press people too hard under these circumstances. They would only regret and recant what they had said earlier. He placed himself diagonally behind her.

"You do know that Anton didn't want to tell us where the first break-in was planned?" he asked.

"I know."

"And," continued DeKok, "if Anton finds ut that you talked to the police, you could get into a lot of trouble."

She nodded, almost imperceptibly.

DeKok sighed deeply.

"Very well, then, Marie. What does 'Operation Harlequin' mean?"

She turned in her chair and faced him.

"Will Anton stay out of trouble? That's the only reason I'm here, you know."

DeKok looked at her unemotionally.

"Has anything happened yet?"

She worried nervously with a glove in her lap.

"Nossir," she said, shaking her head. "Nothing has happened yet. But believe me, sir, I've been scared stiff all this time. You see, Jan Brets would have done it. I promise you, he would have. He was going to kill the old night watchman with a hockey stick."

10

DeKok could not control an exclamation of surprise.

"What!? A hockey stick?"

Marie nodded in confirmation.

"That's what they were going to use all right, a hockey stick. It was one of Brassel's ideas. According to him, nobody would notice if you happened to be walking around with a hockey stick. You see that all the time, especially on Sunday night."

DeKok rubbed his hands over his lips. The revelations of the young woman confused him. It was as if the veil that hung around the dead harlequin was getting ever larger and more impenetrable. Like a London fog. Jan Brets who was supposed to kill an old watchman with a hockey stick, was himself killed with a hockey stick. Coincidence? It was almost frightful how the figure of Pierre Brassel kept lurking through the mist like an evil shadow.

He sat down again behind his desk and pulled thoughtfully on his lower lip. He let it plop back with a most annoying sound.

"To recapitulate," he said, "Operation Harlequin was to be executed on a Sunday night and a watchman, or guard, was to be killed with a hockey stick."

"Yes."

"Excellent, and where was this to take place?"

She made a helpless gesture.

"I don't know if I remember that correctly," she said hesitatingly, "I didn't pay that much attention, you see. But I think it was Bunsum & Company, or Bunsum, Incorporated, something like that. On Drain Street maybe, yes, Drain Street, at the corner of an alley. Is that possible?"

DeKok nodded.

"That's possible, yes, quite possible. I know which company you mean. It's definitely Bunsum."

She sighed a sigh of relief.

"I thought I'd forgotten."

DeKok smiled.

"Did you hear which Sunday was planned?"

She gestured toward a calendar on the wall.

"Now, this coming Sunday. Jan had gone ahead to look the place over. Mainly the outside, you know. Brassel was going to give him everything he needed for the inside."

"Do you know what they were after?"

"No."

"Apart from Anton and Jan, were any others involved?"

She gave him a tired smile.

"I think so, but I really don't know any more." It sounded like an apology.

DeKok placed his hand on her arm in a reassuring gesture.

"Marie," he said in a friendly tone of voice, "believe me, you have helped us a lot."

A worried look came over her face.

"And Anton? What about Anton?"

DeKok's eyebrows moved in that inimitable ripple.

"I," he said, placing his hand on his chest, "I have nothing against Anton. I don't need him for anything. I'll make sure that the break-in at Bunsum & Company will not succeed. That's all." He raised a cautioning finger. "But," he continued in a compelling voice, "you go back to Utrecht and take care of Anton. You said so yourself. Anton likes to have other people think for him. Well, Jan Brets is dead."

It took a while to sink in. Then a spark of understanding lit up her green eyes. The worried look dissipated slowly from her face and it was transformed by a relieved laugh.

"Dammit, yes!" she exclaimed vehemently. "I'll do the thinking from now on. All of it! You can say that again!"

"That!" said DeKok with a smile.

* * *

As soon as Marie had left, DeKok grabbed the telephone and called the desk sergeant.

"I'd like extra surveillance for Bunsum & Company on Drain Street, from now until Monday night. I don't think anything will happen, but I want it covered. There's a plan to break in and to kill the old guard, there, if he's in the way."

"I'll have the necessary personnel assigned."

"Thank you."

DeKok replaced the receiver. Vledder stood next to him, a piece of paper in his hand.

"I have here," said the younger man businesslike, "a synopsis, or rather, a conclusion, based on the facts as we now know them. Of course, that includes the information from Marie Sailmaker."

DeKok nodded thoughtfully.

"Marie," he sighed, "I hope she can control Fat Anton. She really seems to love that lump of flesh."

"May I," interrupted Vledder impatiently, "may I present my . . ."

"Yes, yes." DeKok's thoughts seemed far away.

Vledder cleared his throat.

"All right, then," said Vledder. "Pierre Brassel, respected accountant, obtains confidential information regarding Bunsum & Company. This information probably includes the knowledge regarding a large amount of cash on the premises. What is his next step? He goes to Utrecht and contacts Jan Brets, a well-known burglar. He proposes that Brets empties the safe, or whatever, . . . eh, wherever the cash is kept and . . ."

". . . and Jan Brets agrees," completed DeKok. "He thinks it's a wonderful idea and is very flattered that Mister Brassel was so kind as to pick him, from among all the well-known underworld figures who could just as easily have taken care of the job. And that includes knocking down an old watchman. Anyway, Jan Brets immediately contacts his nearest and dearest and settles on Fat Anton, who likes the idea as well. Together they wait for further orders from Brassel, the brain and . . ."

". . . and Brassel," completed Vledder in turn, "orders Brets to take lodgings in the Greenland Arms. That way he will be closer to the scene and will have an opportunity to spy out the lay of the land. And although not everything seems to have been decided, the tentative date for the robbery has been set for this coming Sunday."

DeKok made a grand gesture.

"There you are, then," he said with false gaiety, "that's it. Everything is completely logical. Just another criminal conspiracy to drain the cash from Bunsum & Company at the Drain Street."

Vledder shook his head emphatically.

"It's not at all logical," he objected. "Not at all. Because, you see, even before the burglary can come to fruition, Pierre Brassel writes you an idiotic note and allows Brets, who was after all supposed to do the actual robbery, allows Brets to be murdered in his hotel room." He snorted audibly. "DeKok, there isn't anything logical about it."

DeKok nodded.

"Yes, indeed, Dick," he agreed pleasantly, "you're right. Everything together like that is anything but logical if . . ." He did not complete the sentence, but rubbed his hands through his hair.

Vledder looked at him with surprise.

"If what?"

With a deep sigh DeKok rose from his chair and placed a fatherly hand on the young man's shoulder.

"I've told you before," he said chidingly, "be careful with intelligent people. The patterns we design, they've already inspected and rejected."

"What's that supposed to mean?"

DeKok shook his head.

"It means nothing at all, at all. No more than what I say. Be careful, don't jump to conclusions. Don't be blinded by what seems to be true. The most obvious is not necessarily the right answer."

"What *do* you mean?" Vledder seemed totally mysti- fied.

"Let's give it a rest for now," DeKok answered a bit impatiently. "I propose we first get a few hours sleep. I don't know how you feel, but I'm bone tired."

He thought for a while, then he said:

"It would seem best for you to go to Bunsum & Company, tomorrow morning. You won't rest anyway, until you've spoken personally to the manager. Then you inquire tactfully about the amount of cash they keep on the premises. If possible you give him a friendly hint to change accountants. We'll see each other again, here in the office, at about noon. Make sure you bring the watchman with you."

"Bunsum's night watchman?"

"Yes, I want to talk to him."

"Why?"

DeKok was becoming visibly upset.

"Because," he exclaimed angrily, "I don't know what in blazes is going on!"

They put their coats on an walked down the long corridor to the stairs. DeKok felt his feet starting to hurt. It was a bad sign, he knew. His feet always hurt when things did not progress satisfactorily. With some difficulty he stumbled down the stairs. Young Vledder was walking in front of him. Outside, in front of the station, DeKok called him back.

"In a little while," he remarked nonchalantly, "if you happen to have a few spare minutes before going to sleep ..."

"Yes, so what?"

"I would like you to think about an interesting question."

Vledder looked absent mindedly at his mentor.

"Question?"

DeKok nodded.

"Yes, *why* was Jan Brets murdered?"

* * *

A bit lost, DeKok ambled through Utrecht. He felt like a fish out of water. He did not like to leave Amsterdam. He preferred to operate in Amsterdam where he knew every street, every alley, every canal. Utrecht was strange territory. All he really knew about Utrecht was that it had the highest Cathedral in Holland. He looked around. The canals, he found, did not compare favorably to the canals in Amsterdam. The bridges were too high and the windows were too low. It was almost like a foreign country, he thought bitterly.

His old felt hat on the back of his head, his ever present raincoat over one arm, he ambled along, reading the street signs as he passed. With a strange feeling of alienation, he finally reached the Servet Street. Cynthia Worden lived in that street. Number 271228 was her phone number and she had talked to Jan Brets. Idly he wondered what sort of a woman she was. Jan Brets had called her twice from the Greenland Arms. Was she his lover?

The Servet Street was a narrow street in the shadow of the Cathedral that dominated the skyline of Utrecht. DeKok passed a few small shops and stopped in front of a door, embellished with a red, plastic sign. *Cynthia Worden*, he read, and below: *Photographic Model*. With his little finger he rubbed the bridge of his nose and with the other hand he rang the doorbell.

There was no response to his ring. Nobody opened the door. He looked at the clock tower. Almost nine-thirty; too early for a photo model? What time did those people go to bed? Again he pressed the doorbell and kept his finger on it. After a while he placed one ear against the door and listened. Faintly he could hear the buzz of the doorbell from the inside. Otherwise all was silent.

Carefully DeKok looked around. People in the Servet Street were busy, he noticed. Much too busy to pay a lot of attention to a middle aged man with a friendly face and a ridiculous hat, who constantly rang the same doorbell.

He searched his pocket for the small tool that had belonged to Handy Henkie's instrument case. It consisted of a brass tube, the size of a pocket knife, which enclosed a number of telescoping, adjustable steel pins and what looked like the beards of keys. DeKok had gained a certain expertise with the innocent looking tool. Shielded by his raincoat, he felt for the lock. It did not take long. Within two minutes the door was open. The hinges squeaked slightly as he pushed the door further open.

After having closed the front door, he stood and listened for a while, just inside the door. Not a sound. The squeaking of the door had not elicited a response. Carefully, balancing on his toes, he walked down the hall. It was remarkable to see how silently, almost floating, he could move his big, heavy body. From a distance it looked like magic. Following an undefinable impulse, he passed the first door, but stopped in front of the second. Softly he tried the handle. It moved. The door was not locked. With one hand on the doorknob, he suddenly realized how Jan Brets had died. It had been a quick death. It must have happened almost immediately after he innocently entered the room. Because behind the door a man was waiting, an unknown man with a reinforced hockey stick. DeKok grinned silently to himself. Perhaps he was now in the same predicament. Except, he was not as unweary as Brets. Forewarned is forearmed, he thought. He carefully stepped back, turned the knob and pushed the door slightly. Just a little too fast. The door flew open wide and slammed against something. Every muscle in DeKok's body tensed. The open door revealed a nebulous twilight, without form, without color. A sensual scent of perfume wafted toward the open door. That was all.

Slowly his eyes adjusted to the gloom. The room he was looking into, took shape, took on dimensions. He discovered a large, wide canopy bed in the center of the room. Gossamer curtains hung down on all sides, enclosing the bed and its occupant. It was a dream, a symphony of pink spun sugar.

Hesitatingly and alert, DeKok slowly stepped into the bedroom. Almost immediately he sensed the overpowering presence of a woman. The surrounding scent made his skin tingle, stimulated his senses. He walked over to the unmade bed and felt the pillows. The pillows were still warm. Until moments ago, somebody had been in the bed for an extended period of time.

His alertness increased. The man, or woman, who had slept in the bed, could not be far away. His sharp gaze roamed around the room. He did not see a hiding place anywhere. Nowhere?

Suddenly he stepped back and smiled.

"I would come out from under the bed," he said pleasantly. "It must be uncomfortable. Also, it's probably dusty."

It took a few seconds. Then a female head with long, blonde, mussed hair emerged from underneath the bed. The head turned. The eyes stared at the flat feet of the policeman. With amusement DeKok observed how the astonishment on the face increased gradually.

"How did you get in, who are you, where are you from?"

DeKok laughed.

"Those are three questions at once. I never answer more than one question."

She stared at him from her position on the floor.

"What are you doing here?"

DeKok did not answer directly. His mind was busy with something else. He also wondered about the strange perspective from which she was looking at him. It must be a comical sight for her.

"Why don't you," he proposed, "come out from under the bed. That way we can continue the conversation at a more normal level. This can be a bit tiring."

She sighed audibly.

"You will have to leave a moment. I'm not dressed."

DeKok made a decision.

"Just tell me where your clothes are. I'll hand them to you and I'll turn around while you put them on."

He saw her hesitate.

"I *promise*," he said with a winning smile. "Believe me, that still means something to men of my age."

She stretched a slender arm toward a low bench in front of a dressing table.

"My robe."

DeKok picked up the desired article of clothing and tossed it in her direction. Then he turned his back discreetly. A few seconds later she walked by him on bare feet. A good looking woman, no taller than his shoulders.

"Come into the living room," she said. Her voice was devoid of any kind of accent.

She walked in front down the corridor. DeKok followed complacently. Meanwhile he admired her supple figure. Although giving the appearance of ethereal fragility, she was not skinny, as so many models often are. On the contrary, her figure seemed pleasantly filled in all the right places.

In contrast to the bedroom, the living room was drenched in daylight. The only barrier between the interior and the outside world consisted of some sheer curtains in front of the windows. The decor was modern and showed taste. Modern paintings, mainly consisting of bizarre color combinations, managed to impart a cheerful atmosphere.

Cynthia Worden curled up like a cat in a sort of hammock on legs and gestured DeKok toward a wide bench, without armrests. She seemed completely at ease. DeKok looked at her searchingly, looking for signs of decline, but could not find any. The daylight was no disadvantage to her beauty.

"How did you get in?"

"I rang," answered DeKok.

She nodded.

"I heard that. You are, how shall I say it, rather tenacious."

"When you didn't answer, I came in. The front door," he lied, "was not locked." He ignored her astonished gaze. "Perhaps I should introduce myself," he continued. "My name is DeKok, with kay-oh-kay. I'm a police inspector from Amsterdam. I've been assigned the investigation regarding the death of Jan Brets."

He saw a shock go through her. Her alluring, almost tempting, pose was immediately forgotten.

"You're from Homicide?"

The corners of her mouth trembled. She stood up from her hammock and grabbed a pack of cigarettes. Then, changing her mind, she threw the pack down again and fiddled with a cigarette lighter. She seemed to have lost her composure.

"What do you want from me?"

Her voice sounded scared.

"Just a bit of information, is all," said DeKok. "For instance, what was the victim to you? What was your relationship?"

"Well, there was no question of an affair."

"Tell me what to call it."

"What?"

"Your relationship with Jan Brets."

She sat down again in the hammock. Very chaste, the robe tight around her knees.

"We were friends."

DeKok nodded.

"All right," he said resignedly. "You and Brets were friends. Excellent, really excellent. Therefore I can assume that you don't mourn his death, isn't that right? After all, that's common, isn't it ... among friends?"

She looked sharply at him, trying to gauge if he was joking. But his face only showed utter sincerity.

"Well," she said finally. "we weren't really *close* friends."

"Yet he called you twice, shortly before his death?"

"Yes."

"Why?"

The corners of her mouth trembled again.

"Just conversations, nothing special."

DeKok pressed his lips together. He did not feel like conducting a long and laborious interrogation. Time was short. He had to be back in Amsterdam by noon.

"Now, you listen to me," he said sternly. "As a rule I couldn't care less about the conversations between young men and women. But Jan Brets is dead. Somebody bashed in his skull and I want to know the who and wherefore, Miss Cynthia. Also, I would like another explanation from you, for instance, about your comic behavior, a little while ago, under the bed."

She did not answer, but lowered her head. DeKok suddenly noticed that she was crying. A few tears dropped

106

on the hands in her lap. DeKok resisted the urge to get up and place a protective arm around her shoulder. He would have liked to do it. But he remained seated, outwardly unmoved. In such a short time he had seen her in too many, quickly changing moods. It made him suspicious. Patiently he waited until she had dried her tears. When she looked up again he saw that she had cried real tears. He let her be, waited until she spoke of her own accord.

"I'm afraid, Inspector," she said after a long pause. "It probably would be best if I told you everything honestly. Really, I'm afraid for my life. When you opened the door of my bedroom, a little while ago, I thought I had breathed my last."

Her voice was now calm, without emotion. Her pose had gone. Her big, blue eyes were serious.

"Is that why you crawled under the bed?"

She nodded.

"I thought it was *him*!"

"Who?"

"Freddy Blaken." She sighed deeply. "A former boyfriend of mine."

"Well, what of it?"

The expression on her face changed. There was total, unadulterated fear in her beautiful blue eyes. She stretched her arms toward DeKok beseechingly.

"You must catch him," she uttered wildly, distraught. "As soon as possible. You must arrest him before he comes back here. He killed Jan Brets!"

11

DeKok raked his fingers through his hair. The wild accusation from Cynthia had not shocked him in the least. Experience had shown that those types of statements should be taken with a large grain of salt. He was suspicious of spontaneous allegations. They were usually the product of suppressed emotions, more hunch than reason.

He looked at the young photo model. She sat before him, shivering in her robe, a frightened child. He suddenly realized that her face was familiar. With surprise he remembered having seen her face hundreds of times, laughing cheerfully from up-beat advertisements on billboards, in the papers, in magazines. He grinned bitterly. The way he saw her now, was not an example of exuberant joyfulness.

"Why don't you put on something warmer?" he ordered. "You don't have to be tempting, or beautiful, or provocative for me. I'm just a civil servant with the soul of a petty official." He made a sad gesture, pointing at her. "All that is just wasted on me."

A faint smile brightened her face momentarily.

"Just a moment, then," she said and left the room.

She returned within minutes, dressed in jeans, a thick, formless sweater and a pair of slippers that resembled full-size rabbits. She had also found time to brush her hair. It framed her face in glorious waves. She was one of those people that could be dressed in sackcloth and still be striking.

"So," said DeKok, when she had seated herself again, "Freddy Blaken killed Jan Brets?"

"Yes."

"Why?"

She pulled her head between her shoulders.

"Because of hate, jealousy."

DeKok nodded.

"The same feeling of hate, of jealousy, prompts him to seek your death?"

"Yes."

Thoughtfully DeKok pulled on his lower lip.

"Well," he said with a sigh, "if Freddy's love for you was in proportion to his hate at the moment, he must have loved you a lot."

Her blue eyes locked with his. The tone of mockery in his voice had not escaped her.

"There are witnesses," she said sharply. It sounded like a reproach.

"Witnesses?"

"Yes. There are plenty of people who heard Freddy say so. 'First I'll break that clown's skull and then I'll come after you,' he said."

DeKok sat closer to the edge of the bench. He seemed suddenly very much interested.

"Clown?"

"Yes."

DeKok looked at her with amazement.

"He called Jan Brets a *clown*?" he asked.

She nodded emphatically.

"Clown, or joker. You see, Freddy couldn't stand it that Jan was the life of the party. Any party. Afterwards Freddy used to curse. He didn't like Jan, thought he was a show-off." Her tone of voice changed. "And Jan *was* fun. He was a fun guy. That's why I went with him."

DeKok sighed. The eternal triangle, he thought.

"And you left Freddy for that?"

"Yes, Freddy was always too serious, I mean moody and somber. Finally I couldn't stand it any more."

"When was the final break?"

She did not answer at once. She finally succumbed and lit up a cigarette. She inhaled deeply, as one who has quit and started again.

"I've been avoiding Freddy for the last few days," she said through a cloud of smoke. "I just happened to meet him again recently, in a bar. That was the day before yesterday. I told him it was over between us, that I was dating Jan and that he didn't have to come back." She sighed, crushing her cigarette after only a few puffs. "It developed into quite a row."

DeKok nodded.

"And then, furious, he said he would kill Jan and you?"

"Yes."

"So, that was on the day of the murder?"

Her head barely moved in assent.

"Yes, on the day of the murder," she repeated tonelessly.

They remained silent. Outside in the Servet Street they heard a car honk and a child yelled something.

"Well, it does appear," said DeKok after a pregnant silence, "that Freddy made good on his promise as far as Jan Brets is concerned."

He spoke more to himself than to the young woman. Pensively he rubbed his hands over his face. His thoughts built an image. He tried to imagine what had happened in the Greenland Arms.

"How did Freddy know," he asked suddenly, "where to find Jan Brets?"

"How? But they were in the syndicate together." There was surprise in her voice.

DeKok's eyebrows rippled briefly.

"What syndicate?"

"Yes, well, a syndicate, an organization to ..." She stopped talking. Then went on: "I don't really know if I'm supposed to talk about it."

DeKok looked at her evenly.

"Jan is dead," he said flatly.

"You're right," she agreed, "it doesn't matter anymore." She moved a blonde lock of hair out of her eyes with an elegant, yet routine, gesture. It seemed as if she realized for the first time that one of her friends had died. Her blue eyes were moist.

"Jan," she whispered, "was approached by somebody from Amsterdam. It was a man who was apparently well versed in the business world. He asked Jan to build an organization in Utrecht, a syndicate to execute planned burglaries."

"But why in Utrecht?"

She shrugged her shoulders.

"I think the man said something about Utrecht being centrally located, good connections, roads, you know. After all, we *are* in the center of the country. Anyway, he thought it would be easier to operate from Utrecht than from Amsterdam, or Rotterdam, for instance."

"Go on."

"Jan liked the idea and went in search of partners. He knew Freddy Blaken from before. About two weeks ago he stopped by to ask Freddy if he wanted to join."

"And?"

"Freddy was interested and Jan became a regular visitor."

DeKok sighed.

"With fatal consequences?"

She nodded.

"I liked Jan a lot better than Freddy, almost from the start. He was so much more cheerful. Freddy warned me about Jan, told me to stay away from him. According to Freddy, Jan was dangerous, a brute, with at least one murder on his conscience." She smiled indulgently. "But Freddy was jealous."

DeKok nodded slowly.

"And jealous people ..." He did not complete the sentence, but asked: "Do you know if the syndicate has completed any operations?"

"No, I don't think so. Everything was still in the planning stages."

"Do you know any other participants? Have you ever heard the name Fat Anton?"

Slowly she shook her head.

"I've never heard of any others."

"The man from Amsterdam, do you know him?"

Again she shook her head.

"I don't know him. I just heard his name, once or twice. It was Brasser, Brassel, something like that. I don't know exactly."

113

DeKok took a deep breath.

"Listen to me, this is important: Do you know of any other people who called Jan Brets a clown, or a joker?"

She waved vaguely with her hands.

"Freddy was the only one."

DeKok remained silent for a long time. Then he picked up his hat from the floor and rose slowly to his feet.

"Come on," he ordered, "put on something more suitable. You're coming with me."

Taken aback, she looked at him.

"With you?"

DeKok gestured impatiently.

"You certainly don't expect me to leave you alone in the house, while Freddy walks around with murder on his mind?" He shook his head emphatically. "No, my dear girl, out of the question. You're coming to Amsterdam with me. I know of a small, friendly hotel where you can hide out for a while. It's safer for you and better for my peace of mind."

She voiced a number of objections, but finally she stood up to change. She walked to a large built-in closet and searched through her outfits. From over her shoulder DeKok looked on critically. He saw a number of strange hats and a wider variety of exuberant, minuscule dresses. It made him uneasy. The friendly creases around his mouth formed a worried look.

"Please keep it decent," he said with small-minded conservatism. "People already look at me strangely."

12

"What's your opinion of Cynthia Worden?" Young Vledder had listened intently to DeKok's report about the events in Utrecht. His brain tried to assimilate the new information with what they already knew. The new developments, he thought, opened a number of fresh perspectives. "Can you trust her, you think?" he asked.

DeKok made a helpless gesture.

"What do you mean by trust?" he asked carefully. "For myself, I believe she spoke the truth."

"So, Freddy Blaken really threatened Brets?"

"Oh, yes, no doubt about that. I even assume there were witnesses who will testify under oath."

Vledder spread both arms.

"Well," he said impatiently, "what are we waiting for?"

DeKok looked at him, cocking his head to one side.

"What do you want to do?"

"Arrest Blaken, what else?"

"On what grounds?"

"Murder."

"Oh."

Vledder slapped his hands flat on the desk.

"Yes," he cried enthusiastically, "he's the man we're looking for. Just think. We couldn't understand why Brets was murdered. There was no motive. Well, here's the motive: jealousy and hate. We didn't know why the corpse was placed in that strange harlequin position. Well, here's the explanation: Freddy called him a clown, he made him look like a clown." He looked seriously at his mentor. "It all fits!" he continued. "Freddy Blaken hated Brets so much that he wanted to insult him, even in death. That's why he made him into a harlequin. You see what I mean, he made a statement: Jan Brets, the clown, is dead."

A strange silence fell on the room. The last words of the young inspector echoed around the bare walls. It was as if the death of Brets had become tangible; a murder with dimensions. DeKok pushed his lower lip forward.

"Jan Brets," he said tonelessly, "clown unto death." He looked encouragingly at his protege. "Clever," he added, admiringly, "very clever. A great theory. My compliments."

Dick Vledder looked at him, a look of suspicion in his eyes. He listened for a tone of sarcasm in DeKok's voice, but it was not there. The admiration of his older colleague seemed sincere.

"But it won't be easy," continued DeKok, "to find Freddy Blaken. I asked her specifically, but Cynthia didn't know where he could be. Anyway, she's scared stiff of her former boyfriend. I had to assure her several times that she would be safe in the hotel."

"And is she?"

DeKok sighed deeply.

"It seemed the only solution. What else could I do? I could hardly give her a police escort, not with the shortage of personnel. And it just wouldn't do to place her in protective custody. I don't think she belongs in jail. But, as long as our Cynthia doesn't show herself in the street, that hotel is the safest place for her. I know the owner. He'll keep an eye on her. Also, she isn't registered under her own name. She's been registered as Mrs. Vledder."

Vledder looked at him wide eyed.

"Why Mrs. Vledder?" he asked irritated.

DeKok shrugged his shoulders nonchalantly.

"What does it matter? I couldn't think of anything else, at the time. Anyway, you could do worse for a wife. Cynthia is really beautiful."

Vledder looked daggers at him.

"Beautiful or not," he growled, "I don't like it. From now on, use your own name for that sort of thing. If Celine discovers there's already a Mrs. Vledder ..."

DeKok laughed heartily.

"Aha," he joked, "so, *that's* the problem!"

Vledder snorted.

"There's no problem," he exclaimed, "but I would like to draw your attention to the fact that an old man has been waiting for you for more than an hour.

"An old man?"

Vledder nodded.

"The night watchman from Bunsum in the Drain Street. He had to be here by noon, you said. Remember?"

DeKok gripped his head with both hands.

* * *

The man looked very neat. He wore a brown corduroy suit with leather patches on the elbows. He did not look at all like a night watchman. He looked more like a Bohemian, with long, wavy hair and a well trimmed beard. His brown eyes darted restlessly around.

117

DeKok apologized sincerely.

"I'm very sorry," he said, "that I've kept you waiting so long. You have every right to complain about my behavior. To be completely honest, I'd forgotten all about you. It simply slipped my mind. I'm so sorry, please excuse me."

The old man laughed.

"To be truly repentant," he said, "is no shame. It's therefore remarkable how seldom it happens."

DeKok looked closely at the old man. He detected both spirit and education in the voice. It surprised him.

"You're a night watchman?" he asked tentatively.

The old man nodded cheerful assent.

"For Bunsum in Drain Street."

"How long have you been doing that?"

"About two years. Ever since my wife died." The old man looked sadly in the distance. "It was necessary," he continued, "I simply had to find something to do, or I would have died too. My daughter was right. 'Papa,' she said, 'find something to do. You're just pining away.' She introduced me to the younger Bunsum." He smiled shyly. "That's how I became a night watchman." He paused. "You see," he continued, "it suits us both very well. When I come home in the morning, I fix her breakfast and call her in time to go to the office. I sleep while she's at work and she sleeps while I'm at work. It's almost an ideal arrangement. We get along just fine, my daughter and I."

DeKok nodded.

"What was your profession before you became a night watchman?"

The old man pulled his beard while he answered.

"Teacher, I taught industrial arts, mechanical drawing, to be exact."

"Oh?"

"Yes, it's a bit different. But I had to retire, you see, at sixty five. I'm almost seventy now, just a few more months."

DeKok showed his admiration.

"Well, you certainly don't look it," he said, "you look very fit."

The old man beamed.

"Well, I am. I can still take care of myself."

DeKok nodded slowly. He wondered if the old man was fit enough to deal with a reinforced hockey stick. He did not think so.

"You ever have any problems, at night?"

"Oh, no. There isn't all that much worth taking, I think. Actually, I'm less of a watchman, at night, than a handyman. I like to keep busy and I fix things."

"But the firm finds it necessary to have a guard at night?"

"Yes."

"Do you work Sundays?"

The old man nodded emphatically.

"Certainly, quite a few week-ends."

"Including this coming Sunday?"

A smile lit up the old man's face.

"No," he said, shaking his head, "as it happens, not this coming Sunday."

"You have a replacement?"

Again the old man shook his head.

"No, no replacement. This coming Sunday there won't be anyone on duty."

DeKok's eyebrows started one of their amazing dances. The old man watched in fascination.

"No guard," questioned DeKok, "but . . ."

"Oh, it doesn't matter, once in a while. Young Bunsum thought the same when I asked him. After all, it would be

119

rather coincidental if something were to happen just when I'm not there."

DeKok swallowed.

"B-but," he stuttered, "*why* won't you be there this Sunday?"

The old man's eyes sparkled.

"My daughter and I," he said, "have both been invited to a party."

"A party?" asked DeKok.

The old man nodded emphatically.

"Yes, my daughter is a secretary for Brassel & Son, CPAs. Her boss, Mr. Brassel is throwing a party for the personnel at his house, next Sunday. He invited me as well."

DeKok rubbed his face with both hands. It was an extremely weary gesture. Finally he found his voice again.

"I think," he said tiredly, "that I have enough information for the moment, Mr. . . . . eh, . . ."

"Petersma," supplied the old man.

DeKok smiled politely.

"Mr. Petersma, thank you very much for coming to see me and once again, my sincerest apologies for having kept you waiting."

The old man stood up and walked toward the door.

"Just one more question," called DeKok, "when did you get the invitation to the party?"

The old man reflected a moment.

"Two weeks ago," said Mr. Petersma.

* * *

With his head in his hands, both elbows resting on the desk, DeKok stared into the distance. He seemed dazed. His normally somewhat good-natured, slightly sad expression had turned weary. He felt as if he was sinking deeper and deeper into a whirlpool of confusion. His brain worked at top speed. Restlessly it looked for a point of reference, a handhold, a starting point. Vledder took a chair and placed it across from him.

"So, Brassel's lovely secretary, the green-eyed brunette with the irresistible dimple on her cheek, is the daughter of Bunsum's night watchman."

DeKok grinned.

"Exactly, the same night watchman who was destined to be knocked down by Jan Brets during Operation Harlequin. The one for whom the hockey stick was meant."

"But," said Vledder, with wonder, "but there's something that doesn't compute! There would be no watchman for Brets to knock down."

DeKok nodded slowly.

"You're right, Dick, it doesn't compute. The so carefully prepared hockey stick is superfluous. The watchman was never meant to be there. He's been invited to a party."

Vledder swallowed, a sudden lump in his throat.

"A party at Brassel's."

DeKok stood up and started to pace up and down the detective room. He stopped in front of the window and looked outside.

"It's almost a comedy of errors," he said wistfully. "A comic play for our amusement, if . . . Jan Brets had not been killed so thoroughly."

He turned toward Vledder.

"You went to Bunsum, this morning?"

"Yes."

"Well?"

"Nothing."

"What do you mean, nothing?"

Vledder shrugged his shoulders in a careless gesture.

"Exactly what I'm saying. Mr. Bunsum had no idea what a burglar could find worthwhile in his building. There was nothing to steal, he thought. The big money, the real money went straight to the bank. There was only a small amount of petty cash in an old safe."

"What about their accountant?"

"It isn't Brassel."

"No?"

"No."

DeKok's eyebrows rippled. As always, Vledder watched, fascinated. He carefully tried to imitate the movement. As always, he failed.

"But," said DeKok after a long pause, "Brassel's secretary had enough influence with Bunsum & Company to make sure that her father would get a job as night watchman."

Vledder nodded.

"Easy enough, if Brassel cooperated."

"How's that?"

Vledder smiled a secret smile.

"They're friends."

"Who?" DeKok sounded impatient.

"Brassel and Bunsum, they were in Grade School together."

13

It was clearly visible that Inspector Vledder was deep in thought. His youthful face was serious. His chin stuck out and a deep, vertical wrinkle appeared on his forehead. Suddenly his eyes lit up. The chin withdrew and the deep crease disappeared.

"I've got it!" he exclaimed. "It's as clear as day!"

DeKok who was studying a floor plan of the Greenland Arms, looked up absent-mindedly.

"What's clear?"

Vledder sat down across from him.

"Why Brassel invited the watchman to his party."

"Oh yes, why then?"

"Easy," smiled Vledder, "he didn't want the father of his secretary knocked off."

Shaking his head, DeKok looked at Vledder.

"I'm certain," he said, "that it's not exactly as simple as you think. Just think a moment about what Marie Sailmaker told us yesterday. Do you remember how she told us that it had been agreed during the planning in Fat Anton's house to do something about the night watchman? Remember how Brets was supposed to take care of that and how Brassel supposedly suggested that it could best be done with a hockey stick? That was about a week ago! At that time Brassel already *knew* that there would be no guard that night. He had invited the guard a week earlier!"

Vledder groaned as if in pain.

"Dammit, yes," he cried, angry with himself. "You're right. It's true. Petersma had been invited a week earlier, two weeks ago." He stared out the window, chewing his lower lip. "But . . . ," he resumed hesitantly, "but why didn't Brassel say anything? Why did he propose to render the watchman harmless and why did he suggest the hockey stick?"

DeKok raised both arms.

"Yes," he said, exasperated, "why indeed? Why so many things? Why did Brets get killed with the same hockey stick?"

At that moment the phone rang. Vledder picked it up.

"Is this Inspector DeKok?" asked a voice.

"No, one moment." He handed the phone to his partner. "It's for you," he added.

"DeKok here."

"I promised to call you," said the voice at the other end of the line, "if anybody was interested in Mrs. Vledder, the lady you brought over, earlier today."

"Yes."

"There was a man here, a little while ago."

"And he asked for Mrs. Vledder?"

"No, he didn't ask for Mrs. Vledder, but he meant her. He called her something else."

"What?"

"He called her Cynthia, Cynthia Worden."

DeKok threw the receiver down and went over to the peg, to get his coat.

"Come on," he called over his shoulder, "let's hit the road."

"Where to?" asked Vledder surprised.

DeKok was struggling into his coat on the way to the door.

"Hotel Dupont and ... Freddy Blaken."

* * *

The owner-doorman-waiter-chef of Hotel Dupont on the Martyrs Canal quickly dried his hands on a white apron and led the policemen to a seating arrangement in the small lobby.

"It was a good looking young man," he explained, "black hair, good clothes. A little loud, maybe. You know what I mean? Self-consciously macho. Not really well brought up at all. Maybe a bit vulgar. About twenty five, I'd say. He asked to speak to the girl that had checked in this morning. I pretended I didn't understand him and asked him what girl he was talking about. That's when he mentioned the name."

"Cynthia Worden?"

"Yes."

"What next?"

"Nothing, I told him that as far as I knew, there was no Cynthia Worden staying here. I didn't lie. Then he left."

DeKok laughed.

"Did he leave a message, or did he tell you he would be back?"

"No, he didn't. But I'm sure he'll be back. He seemed surprised and asked if there were any other hotels on the Martyrs Canal."

DeKok nodded.

"Where's the girl now?"

"Upstairs, in her room." The hotel owner pointed with his thumb.

The inspectors stood up and walked toward the stairs. Halfway there, DeKok turned around and asked:

"Did our little beauty make any telephone calls, after I left?"

"No, at least not from here. I have no phones in the rooms, just this one, at the desk." The man shook his head. "I would have seen her," he added.

"Did she leave at all?"

"Just a minute, to get some cigarettes. Maybe a few minutes."

DeKok nodded thoughtfully. He walked a few steps back and stopped in front of the hotel owner, hand on his chin.

"If our visitor returns," he said, groping for words, "while my colleague and I are upstairs, ask him if he means a blonde girl with blue eyes. If he admits that, and I'm sure he will, bring him upstairs. Knock three times in quick succession on the door, wait a few seconds, then open the door and shove him inside. We'll take it from there."

The hotelier nodded.

"What if he doesn't want to come upstairs," he asked.

"Don't worry, he'll come up."

* * *

Beautiful Cynthia was not happy at all to see Vledder and DeKok enter her room. On the contrary, there was a definite expression of disappointment on her attractive face. DeKok gave her a friendly grin.

"We're here to protect you," he said cheerily. "We got a tip that Freddy Blaken has been spotted in the neighborhood. Apparently he's looking for you. He asked for you downstairs, not too long ago."

She did not react immediately. Seemingly DeKok's announcement did not touch her. She darted a furtive glance at the inspectors, but there was no sign of fear.

"We're happy to see you're still alive," continued DeKok in the same cheerful tone. "If I hadn't given the owner such clear instructions . . ." He paused and sneaked a look at the expression on her face. " . . . we might have been . . . too late," he concluded with a mournful voice.

Her eyes narrowed.

"You're spying on me," she yelled at him.

DeKok shook his head.

"Not at all, at all," he answered calmly. "I've just taken some necessary precautions. That's all. Also, you told me that you had no idea about Blaken's whereabouts. So, how was I to know you would contact your own murderer."

"I didn't contact him."

DeKok's eyebrows vibrated briefly.

"But didn't you phone him this morning to tell him where to find you?"

She avoided DeKok's eyes and lowered her head. Her blonde hair closed off her face as if a curtain had been drawn.

"Didn't you phone?" insisted DeKok.

"Yes."

"Strange behavior for a prospective victim."

She raised her head slowly. The blonde curtain opened up. Her big, blue eyes looked at him. They were moist and a tear rolled down her cheek.

"I want to make it up, between Freddy and me," she whispered. "You understand, Mr. DeKok, I wanted to make up before it was too late and you'd arrest him." She sighed deeply. "After all," she went on, "he did it all for me. Just for me. Because he loved me. I only realized that after I had already betrayed him."

DeKok rubbed his face with a flat hand. Between his fingers he looked at her intently. He was not sure of himself. Love and women, he knew, was a combination fraught with quickly changing emotions, where all logic was out of the question and any intelligent approach was doomed to failure from the start. He thought briefly about his own wife. He had never been able to discover why she loved him.

"Is that why you asked him to come here?" he asked the girl.

She nodded slowly.

"To talk it over," she said listlessly.

DeKok pushed his hat slightly forward and scratched the back of his neck.

"So you *did* know where to reach him?"

"I only had a phone number, in Utrecht."

DeKok grimaced.

"Weren't you afraid," he asked sarcastically, "that he would hurt you? Only this morning you crawled underneath the bed when you didn't even know for sure if it was him."

A sad smile hovered around her lips.

"This morning, yes." She sighed as if a century had passed since then. "But now I've changed my mind, I'm no longer afraid. If you hadn't alerted the man downstairs and Freddy had come here, then I would have told him what I wanted to say. That I still love him and that the affair with Jan Brets was nothing but a mistake." She crushed the collar of her dress between nervous fingers. "Then it would have been up to him," she said with another deep sigh.

The expression on Vledder's face was a mixture of painful surprise and embarrassed disbelief.

128

"And then you would have just waited to be killed?" he asked incredulously. He snapped his fingers. "Just like that? Like love-me-or-kill-me?"

As if in a daze she stared past him and nodded.

"You're crazy," he spat vehemently. "Certifiable! That's not love. That has nothing to do with love, that's . . ."

He was interrupted by three knocks on the door, in quick succession. DeKok shoved Vledder to one side and sprang away himself, out of view from whoever would enter the room. At almost the same moment the door flew wide open. A powerfully built young man stood on the threshold. His dark eyes looked into the room.

A moment of paralysis followed, a pause in the action that lasted no longer than a split second. During that one instant, that single heartbeat when Freddy Blaken stood eye to eye with his former love, hesitating what to do next, in that twinkling of an eye, Cynthia screamed.

It was a short, sharp scream that bounced off the walls. It alarmed Freddy considerably. He felt a threat, saw the approaching hands of the inspectors from the corners of his eyes and like lightning he sprang into action. In a flash he had turned around, thrown the hotel owner against the wall and fled down the stairs.

"Grab him!" yelled DeKok.

Vledder went in pursuit.

Freddy Blaken took the stairs in two jumps, raced through the lobby and ran out of the hotel. In passing he threw on old man to the ground and barely escaped an approaching streetcar.

Vledder followed. As soon as he came outside, he saw Blaken turn the corner of the first side street. It was an area regularly patrolled by constables on foot. But they're never around when you want one, thought Vledder. The disappointment slowed him down. He panted and his heart throbbed in his throat. His legs felt like lead. His quarry was at least fifty yards ahead of him and the distance seemed to increase. Blaken ran into one street and out another. When he finally took the time to look around, he could not discover his pursuer anywhere. Reassured, he slowed down. Finally, upon approaching the Damrak, he slowed to a walk, mingled with the crowds and disappeared in the throngs that entered the Central Railroad Station.

14

"So, he escaped?"

Vledder hung his head in shame.

"That guy ran so much faster than me. He fled via the Herring Packer Alley toward the Damrak and must have disappeared in the Central Station. He just vanished in the crowd. Evaporated."

DeKok smiled at the frustrated face of his younger colleague.

"Don't worry about it," he said encouragingly. "We'll get him eventually, either today, or tomorrow. Anyway, I'm not so sure he's the man we want, after all."

Vledder looked at him with surprise.

"You think he's *not* the murderer?"

DeKok shrugged his shoulders.

"I don't know. We would first have to interrogate him at length. You see, the murderer of Brets must satisfy at least *one* very important condition."

"And that is?"

DeKok made an expansive gesture with both hands.

"He must have the kind of relation with Pierre Brassel that would enable Pierre to know that the murder would happen. You see, the murderer *must* have told Brassel about his plans. And not by some wild outcry in a bar, somewhere, as Cynthia told us, but in a calm, detailed conversation. In an atmosphere conducive to careful planning, not a killing on impulse, but with premeditation. Of course, Cynthia may have been flattered to think that one of her lovers killed the other one over her, but Brets was not the victim of a *crime passionnel*." He paused and rubbed the bridge of his nose with his little finger. "Despite the fact that Blaken was the only one to call Brets a clown," he concluded.

Vledder walked over and leaned on the desk.

"You're still worried about the harlequin posture?"

DeKok nodded meditatively.

"I really have no explanation for it." His voice was somber. "But there is such a lot in this case for which I have no explanation. The syndicate, for instance. Too fantastic for my liking, not logical at all, at all. Just think. The first burglary is planned for Bunsum's. Bunsum is a friend of Brassel. A night watchman is scheduled to be knocked off, but Brassel invites the victim to a party. Jan Brets is going to do the actual burglary, but is killed. And Brassel doesn't lift a finger to prevent any of it."

Vledder nodded sadly in agreement, but suddenly his eyes lit up. As if a single spark had set off an entire new thought process.

"You're right," he exclaimed, wildly enthusiastic. Vledder's moods could be as mercurial as the weather, reflected DeKok, not for the first time. "It would not be logical," continued Vledder, speaking rapidly, "if Brassel allowed Brets to be killed, when he needed him for the burglary."

DeKok, still musing about the mood changes, gave him a confused look.

"I don't understand you."

Vledder laughed, triumph in his voice.

"You know," he said, raising a finger in a subconscious imitation of one of DeKok's stock gestures, "you know something? He didn't need Brets at all for the burglary. There wasn't going to be a burglary."

"What!?"

Vledder grinned.

"There wasn't going to be a burglary," he repeated. "There is nothing to be gained by breaking in at Bunsum & Company. We know that. It was everything, except a good target for a rich haul. I think that Brassel was never serious about 'Operation Harlequin'. It wasn't just fantastic, as you said, it was a fantasy. The entire plan, the gang, the so-called syndicate, all of it, was no more than a masquerade. Brassel made it all up. His only purpose was to get Brets into the Greenland Arms. It was a trap."

"A trap?"

Vledder nodded emphatically.

"Pretending he knew about a rich haul, and maybe more to come, Brassel enticed Brets to take lodgings at the Greenland Arms. Brets fell for it. Believe me, it had to be that way. Brets fell into a trap."

Thoughtfully DeKok chewed his lower lip.

"But the question remains: Who killed Brets and why?"

Vledder's face fell.

"You're right," he admitted, downcast, "it really doesn't give us anything new."

DeKok placed a fatherly hand on the young man's wide shoulder.

"But it isn't at all an idle thought," he said, "no, not at all, at all." His voice was encouraging. "I really believe that Brets was enticed into a trap. It really looks that way."

Suddenly he looked piqued. He shook his head and walked away from Vledder. With long strides he started to pace up and down the room. It was always easier to think on his feet. An avalanche of questions needed answers. After about ten minutes, he sat down at his desk and took a blank sheet of paper from a drawer. In the upper left hand corner he wrote the word TRAP in large block letters. He hesitated a moment, pen in hand, and then added a question mark to the word.

It was one of his habits. He had picked up a lot of them over the years. But if something particularly bothered him, he would write it down. To him it seemed as if the question changed from something abstract to a concrete manifestation of his imagination. He stared at the bare word and tapped his middle finger on the center of the paper.

"How did Brassel know?" he asked, irritation evident in his tone of voice. "How did Brassel, a respected citizen, a professional, know about the existence of a man like Brets, a man with a crime sheet as long as your arm?"

He looked up at Vledder.

"And who was so interested in a burglar, that he decided on murder?" He grinned without mirth, still irritated, and gestured toward the piece of paper. "Was it Pierre Brassel? Did the accountant have anything to gain from Brets' death? It's hardly credible."

They remained silent for a long time. DeKok stared at the word TRAP. Vledder was occupied with his own thoughts.

"It doesn't compute," said Vledder after a while, repeating an earlier statement. "There's just no logical connection, anywhere. The only thing that's obvious, at the moment, is that Brassel is involved. Up to his neck, I'd say. There's no doubt about *that*! But when you try to fit him in, anywhere, it just doesn't work. It really comes down to a single question: What's Brassel's involvement in all this?"

DeKok stood up.

"Let's go ask him," he said.

Vledder looked at him, baffled.

"Ask who?"

DeKok grinned.

"The man who seems to have all the answers."

Vledder beamed.

"Brassel?"

"Yes."

* * *

It was a nice house, friendly, made of red bricks with large windows. Just outside the suburbs, between the Airport and Amsterdam, not too far from the main highway, but far enough to give the illusion of "country". The windows were lit up.

DeKok had judged it better to confront the accountant at home, rather than in his office. Offices, according to his experience, were impersonal, characterless. They seldom offered a glimpse into the personality of the user. But a home is often a mirror of the people who live there. That is why he waited until evening.

It was not difficult to find Pierre Brassel. He was, so to speak, on display, in common with the peculiar Dutch habit of never closing curtains, with the exception of, sometimes, bedroom curtains. Tourists often make it a point to walk the streets of Dutch cities, peeking into rooms as they pass by. Nobody takes offense. On the contrary, the Dutch take great pride in their interiors and invite people to look. Entire cities resemble shopping galleries for furniture and decorating styles. The inhabitants go about their normal business, oblivious to the stares of passers-by.

Pierre Brassel was sitting in an easy chair in front of the fireplace. He was reading. Further back in the large room, his wife was seated at a large, round table, engaged in some embroidery. It was a peaceful scene of domestic tranquility and coziness, bathed in a diffused light that suited the image of a respected accountant at leisure.

Although DeKok, like all Dutch people, seldom gave a particular interior a second thought, he felt guilty at this time. He always felt guilty when he peeked into the home of anybody connected with a case. It gave the police an unfair advantage, he thought. His puritanical background tended to trip him up in such cases. He felt that he was intruding on the intimacy of the two people in the house, that he was catching them in the act. But as an excuse he would then use the national habit of the Dutch to reveal the interiors of their houses. "Sometimes," thought DeKok, "I am too complicated for my own good."

He and Vledder looked at the tableau for some time, unobserved in the dark. The scene of a domestic Brassel, feet in slippers, was so far removed from any criminality, especially a murder, that he could not help but think of it all as a possible joke, a practical joke and that anytime now, somebody, probably in the bushes, would start laughing, loud, wholeheartedly, waking up the quiet complacency of the street. What a joke. All the neighbors would come out to laugh at him, DeKok, the crazy inspector of the Amsterdam Police, who suspected their respected and admired neighbor of nefarious activities. He sighed deeply, then he touched Vledder's arm and approached the door. He hesitated for one more moment, then rang the bell.

They did not have to wait long. The door was opened within seconds. A handsome, slender woman faced them. The voluptuous lines of her figure were silhouetted, etched sharply against the light from within the house. The light sparkled in her blonde hair. DeKok wondered for a moment if he had ever met her before, but could not place her. Then he thought cynically that his path, at times, seemed to be literally strewn with beautiful, blonde women. But of course, there were a lot of beautiful blonde women in Holland and a lot of them looked alike.

"Mrs. Brassel?" he asked, lifting his hat politely.

She nodded calmly.

DeKok gave her his most winning smile, it was almost as irresistible as his boyish grin.

"DeKok, DeKok with . . . eh, kay-oh-kay."

She offered her hand in a friendly manner.

"I heard a lot about you," she said simply.

She had a slightly German accent. It sounded pleasant the way she spoke.

"This is my colleague, Vledder."

"How do you do."

The greetings and introductions were conducted in a formal manner. Mrs. Brassel did not seem in the least surprised about the visit from the two policemen. She acted guileless and natural, as if the men had kept a long planned appointment.

"You wish to speak to my husband?"

DeKok nodded and took his hat in his hand.

"Yes, ma'am, that was the purpose of our visit."

She pointed at a coat rack in the hall.

* * *

The long-legged Brassel was the epitome of a cheerful host. He arranged easy chairs in a half circle, placed a few small tables within easy reach and beamed with forthcoming friendliness.

"Coffee?"

Vledder and DeKok readily nodded assent.

Brassel motioned to his wife and she went to the kitchen. DeKok looked after her admiringly until Brassel again required his attention.

"I read somewhere," remarked the accountant airily, "that the police in general and especially the Amsterdam police consider coffee to be one of life's elixirs. One of the tools needed to do the job. Is that right?"

DeKok smiled politely.

"Yes, you might say that. It's a tonic all right. A well of inspiration. Although some people need stronger stimulants for inspiration."

Brassel did not react. He gestured toward the waiting chairs.

"But do sit down, gentlemen," he said with easy urbanity. "My wife will be here with the coffee in a moment and you'll be able to judge *how* coffee should taste. She's of German origin, you know, my wife, and a marvel in the kitchen. People who have eaten at our table, always wonder how I manage to stay so slim." He grinned apologetically. "But apparently, I don't have a tendency for ... eh, ..."

DeKok looked at him mockingly.

"A tendency for what?"

Momentarily something flashed in Pierre's eyes. Then his lips curled into a smile. ". . . for corpulence," he declared.

DeKok grinned.

"That's nice."

Brassel stretched his long legs and leaned comfortably back in his chair. He placed the tips of his fingers against each other.

"The John-Bull type doesn't happen in our family," he continued. "I can indulge myself with my wife's culinary offerings and it will have no effect on me."

Vledder changed position in his chair. The meaningless chatter irritated him in great measure. He preferred to get to the point. His impatient temperament did not like roundabouts. He preferred short-cuts.

"Have you wondered at all," he asked, "why we're here?"

Pierre Brassel looked at the young inspector, a bit absent minded, as if annoyed by the interruption.

"Excuse me?"

A blush appeared on Vledder's face. The unspoken rebuke, the hint of contempt, irritated him even more. He pulled himself forward, to the edge of the chair.

"Do you know why we're here?" he repeated.

Pierre Brassel nodded calmly, unperturbed.

"It seems rather obvious," he expressed with a sigh. "You have a problem with the rather sudden death of Jan Brets in the Greenland Arms. Professionally speaking, of course, because I don't think you're very upset about it, personally. Your investigations in the case have, until now, been rather fruitless. You have no starting point, too few connecting links . . . whatever. But because of my little note, perhaps even more because of my visit to the police station, you are of the opinion that I can name the murderer." His tone of voice was strictly businesslike, as if he were discussing the implications of a Profit and Loss Statement. "Isn't that right?" he asked in conclusion.

Vledder caught his breath.

"Right, that's it," he uttered, "exactly, yes, that's it."

DeKok enjoyed himself silently. He smiled behind his hand. The face of an astonished Vledder was positively comical to watch.

Mrs. Brassel entered and served coffee. She had also changed. She now wore a simple gown of black material that contrasted alluringly with her clear, ivory colored skin. She also served a slice of home-made cake, which elicited a compliment from DeKok.

"Wonderful," he cried out, enchanted. "Extremely fine, I've never tasted anything like it. My wife should have this recipe."

She gave him a sweet smile.

"I'll get it to her," she almost whispered, "before the week is out."

The secretive tone made DeKok look up in surprise. His eyebrows rippled briefly.

"Before the week is out?" he asked.

Pierre Brassel hastily intervened.

"It's a matter of tradition," he said, a little too loud and emphatic. "My wife is from a very old German family. The special recipes in the family have been handed down from mother to daughter."

DeKok nodded his admiration.

"A fine tradition," he said, "worth maintaining."

Mrs. Brassel smiled dejectedly.

"There are other traditions in our family that . . ." She stopped suddenly. There was a warning in her husband's eyes. A warning that did not escape DeKok. He looked at her with new interest.

"What sort of traditions, Mrs. Brassel?"

She glanced at her husband and sighed.

". . . that . . . eh, that are less innocent."

Brassel laughed, but his eyes did not join in.

"I'm sure my wife refers to a few common traditions, farmer's traditions, at least from the Middle Ages. Isn't that so, Liselotte?"

She lowered her head and nodded.

Brassel immediately turned the conversation in a different direction. In some way he was afraid of what his wife might say. Whenever she spoke, he watched her anxiously, followed every word with singular intensity. It was obvious that he preferred to keep the initiative himself. He turned toward DeKok.

"You have," he asked, "found no mistakes yet, during your investigations *after* the fact?" His tone was politely interested.

DeKok shrugged his shoulders.

"That's difficult to answer," he replied thoughtfully. "I'm sure there were mistakes in the murder of Jan Brets. I don't believe in the perfect crime. However, I must admit that I haven't discovered any mistakes yet."

Brassel beamed, obviously pleased with himself.

"But that doesn't mean a thing," added Vledder hastily. "Just because we haven't found any mistakes, doesn't mean that no mistakes have been made."

The accountant shook his head and laughed. It was an insulting, contemptuous laugh. It did not sound pleasant. Again he stretched his long, thin fingers and placed the tips against each other.

"You two," he said with a condescending arrogance, "have a strange way of reasoning. Every form of logic is missing from your statements." He gestured vaguely. "Mistakes," he explained further, "are only mistakes if they are *discovered*. They simply do not exist before that. They are born at the moment of discovery. Undiscovered mistakes have no reality." He paused and grinned. "I hope the gentlemen can follow me?" he asked gratuitously.

DeKok pressed his lips together. Brassel's supercilious manner was getting on his nerves.

"For myself," he said grimly, "there's but one reality: the murder of Jan Brets." He stretched an arm in the general direction of the complacent accountant. "And talking about logic, how do you explain that an intelligent man, a respectable citizen with a charming wife and two young children, can gamble so easily with twenty years of his life?"

Brassel snorted.

"Twenty years? What for?"

DeKok gave him a penetrating look.

"Murder," he said curtly.

Brassel reacted vehemently.

"Twenty years for murder? In Holland?" He laughed insultingly. "Ridiculous and you know it! There's no judge in the country that will give you twenty years, even if you kill a whole village." He paused and took a deep breath. Calmer, he continued: "Anyway, *I* haven't committed any murder."

DeKok grinned broadly.

"Aha, but there's such a thing as complicity, an accomplice before, during, or after the fact."

Brassel stood up abruptly.

"Accomplice? Accomplice?" He took a few long steps toward the bookcase. His normally somewhat pale face was red with emotion. "Here!" he exclaimed, pointing at a row of neatly bound books with gold letters on the backs. "Here, I have the complete Criminal Code and all relevant jurisprudence for the last one hundred years. I worked myself through it. Carefully, I promise you that, word for word. I've taken advice from the best legal minds in the country." He stretched a finger in DeKok's direction. "If you can prove complicity from my actions in regard to the murder of Jan Brets, you're a lot smarter than all the lawyers, prosecutors and judges of this century."

Unimpressed, DeKok shrugged his shoulders.

"I'm not a judge, a prosecutor, or a lawyer," he remarked mildly. "I'm just a simple cop. I don't have to prove your complicity. If I only have a simple *suspicion*, I've enough to arrest you." He grimaced. "Of course, the *justification* for such an arrest is a matter for later discussion."

Pierre Brassel was getting visibly upset.

"I know the limits of your authority," Brassel said in a shrill voice. "You cannot arrest me! You can do nothing against me. You haven't the right!" Goaded by DeKok's mocking smile, he went on: "You accuse me of being a murderer and you speak of justice?" He shook his head in disgust.

"Mr. Brassel ... ," DeKok spoke slowly and with a threatening undertone to his voice. ". . you would do well to remember that the only reason you're able to play your amusing little murder games with me, is because you rely on my honesty as a human being and my trustworthiness as a guardian of the Law. I must say, it's especially flattering. There's a hidden compliment there, somewhere. But for the moment, it's *all* that stands between you and incarceration."

Brassel looked at DeKok with suspicion.

"I don't understand," he said softly. "Your honesty ... my freedom?"

DeKok nodded emphatically.

"If you had read the law correctly, you would have known that you had the obligation to warn Brets, one way or the other, that he was about to be murdered."

Brassel smiled a superior smile.

143

"But I have done so," he said, self-assured. "I wrote him a note. You probably found it, under the corpse."

DeKok looked at him with well feigned surprise.

"A note?"

"Yes, a warning note."

DeKok pulled a face which clearly expressed incomprehension.

"I found no note," he lied. "I've never seen a note like that."

Brassel looked at him, disbelief in his eyes.

"But you must have."

DeKok made a helpless gesture.

"I'm sorry," he apologized. "There was no note. I fear that this so-called note exists only in your imagination. Therefore I must conclude that you failed to warn Brets, while you knew that his life was in danger. You leave me no choice. It's a criminal offense."

For the first time Brassel lost his temper. He stood in front of DeKok and looked down at him. His hands shook and there were deep red spots on his cheeks.

"You did find it," he screamed. "You must have found it," he repeated, with special emphasis, like a teacher in front of a particularly stupid classroom. His voice thundered through the room. DeKok remained seated, unmoved. He thoughtfully rubbed the bridge of his nose with a little finger and looked up at the man in front of his chair.

"What's the matter, Mr. Brassel," he asked, sarcasm dripping from his voice. "Aren't you feeling well?"

Pierre Brassel gestured wildly, waved his arms.

"That's low," he spit angrily, "false, mean, underhanded, lying. You have the note. Of course you have the note. You found it under the dead body of Brets. I wrote it and

144

Fre . . ." He stopped suddenly, swallowed the last word as a horrified look appeared on his face.

The red spots of anger had disappeared. All color had drained from his face. He looked pale as a ghost. Mrs. Brassel, too, was thoroughly shocked. But she recovered faster than her husband.

"I believe I understand, Mr. DeKok," she said softly. "You're just trying to scare my husband, aren't you? You *did* find the note?" She spoke sweetly flattering, almost beseechingly. "You just want to let him know that you *could* have said that there was *no* note, that no warning had been given." She sighed deeply. "You could say that if you were a dishonest person."

The door opened at that moment and a darling little girl of about six entered hesitantly. She wore light blue pajamas and long ringlets of blonde hair spiraled from her head down to below her shoulders. She rubbed the sleep from her eyes with tiny fists.

"*Ich kann nicht schlafen,*" she said, softly whining in German, "*soviel Schall!*"*

Mrs. Brassel sprang up, went to the child and led her out of the room with softly soothing words.

The short interruption had given Pierre the opportunity to regain his composure. He sat down again and color came slowly back in his face. He rubbed his forehead with the back of his hand.

"The poor child must have been wakened by the noise," he said with a sigh. "But then, you *did* give me a scare."

DeKok ignored the remark.

"Your daughter?" he asked.

Brassel shook his head.

---

* "I can't sleep, so much noise!"

145

"No," he answered, "little Ingrid isn't my daughter. She's my niece, the youngest daughter of my wife's brother. She's just staying with us, visiting. She's a rather nervous child. Very sensitive to surroundings, people around her." He gave a tired smile. "My own children are different. Less vulnerable. They sleep through anything, even an earthquake."

Mrs. Brassel returned after a few minutes. She held an index finger in front of her lips in the international request for silence.

"Ingrid's asleep again," she said. "Please let's be less noisy. The child is such a light sleeper."

She turned toward DeKok.

"The problem of the missing warning note has meanwhile been solved, I hope?"

DeKok nodded.

"I found it," he answered with a smile. "It was indeed underneath the corpse, as your husband guessed."

She sighed a sigh of relief.

"In that case, would you like another cup of coffee?"

Vledder and DeKok nodded in unison.

"What about you, Pierre?"

Brassel looked up, momentarily lost in thought.

"What?"

"Coffee?"

"Coffee . . .? Yes, yes, all right."

DeKok grinned.

"Absent minded, Mr. Brassel? Where were your thoughts? On the pitch?"

Brassel looked at him, incomprehension on his face.

"Pitch?"

"Yes, the pitch, the hockey pitch. After all, it isn't all that long ago that you were the Captain of the University

Hockey Team, was it?" DeKok scratched his ear with an embarrassed gesture. "You were, I think, especially famous for your hit work, your stick technique, on the field." He grinned his irresistible schoolboy grin. "Or do I have the terms wrong? I know little about field hockey."

15

With a moderate speed of less than forty miles per hour, Vledder guided their trusty old VW Beetle back to Amsterdam. They drove along the Amstel river. The dam across the Amstel had created the name and the city of Amsterdam. The river was wide, much wider than normal. Water splashed on the road surface. A sharp, howling wind created whitecaps on the dark water. It was almost scary. More so, reflected Vledder, when one realized that the surface of the river was actually several meters below sea level. On a night like this only the dikes, the sand dunes and the ubiquitous wind mills stood between Holland and total disaster. Dark clouds chased each other along the sky, blotting out the moonlight. A lonely farm house looked like a ghost castle.

DeKok did not pay any attention to his surroundings. He did not see the clouds, or the rain. Little did it matter to him that windmills all over the country were turning like mad under reefed sails to keep the water tables at manageable levels. He did not care that Vledder sometimes had trouble distinguishing between roadway and river surface. He sat in the passenger seat, slumped down, his hat low over his eyes. He yawned thoroughly and with obvious pleasure.

"I'm sleepy," he allowed between two huge yawns. "Let's just stop a moment at the station, just in case, and then we'll go home."

Vledder nodded slowly. His eyes glued to the road. The beam of one of the headlights was not aimed right and gave him less visibility than he would have liked. On the other hand, it did allow him to keep a weary eye on the wild water of the river. As they approached the city, the driving became a little less tense.

"I have a feeling," said Vledder, "as if there's another murder in the offing."

DeKok groaned from underneath his hat.

"One murder is enough for now, thank you very much. Just try to control your feelings."

Vledder laughed.

"Was Pierre Brassel really a hockey player?"

"Yep, a good one too, so I've been told."

"And the stick, I mean the hockey stick that killed Brets, was that one of Brassel's sticks?"

DeKok nodded, but Vledder did not allow his eyes to stray from the road. DeKok, realizing this, said:

"Yes, it belonged to Brassel. The lab found traces of the initials JB in the wood. Apparently it was done years ago, with a pencil. It had worn down, of course, but it was still detectable with the right instruments. No results about the tape, or the lead, yet. I understand there's little to go on. Perhaps they can find out where it came from, but, to tell you the truth, I think that's of less importance."

Vledder sighed deeply, tried to relieve his cramped muscles.

"I don't understand it at all." His tone displayed a certain amount of pique, almost like a spoiled child. "Why anything," he continued. "Brassel's playing with fire. If he

150

didn't happen to have a cast-iron alibi, because of his visit to us, he would have been locked up long ago. I, for one, wouldn't have been at all surprised if he had been convicted for the murder of Brets. Just think of all the evidence we could have offered." He smiled bitterly. "But all that evidence is for nought. We were with him when the murder was committed. There's no getting away from that. We can hardly move the time of death to suit us."

DeKok laughed and pushed his little hat back on his head. With difficulty he raised himself in the seat.

"You know, Dick," said the gray sleuth, looking for words, "that ridiculous note he wrote. That idiotic note asking for an appointment, had only one purpose and that was to provide him with an airtight alibi for a murder he knew was going to be committed and, I'm convinced, he helped prepare himself." He turned in his seat, faced Vledder. "You see, my boy," he continued, "it's especially the last part I don't understand. It bothers me the most."

"How's that?"

"Well, you see . . ." He stopped, raised a finger in front of his eyes and looked at it as if he had never seen it before. ". . . it means that Brassel apparently participated in the preparations *voluntarily*! Certainly he had no objections. He didn't try to stop the killer, no, he extended a helping hand." Again he paused, then: "Why does one commit murder? I mean, premeditated, well prepared murder?" Apparently he had found a use for the finger in front of his face, he added the rest of his fingers and counted on his outspread hand: "Greed, vengeance, jealousy, fear, blackmail."

He lowered his hand, glanced disinterestedly out of the window and shook his head.

"As far as I can determine," he continued his soliloquy, "none of those motives are applicable in this situation. Just think, Brets was as poor as a church mouse. He was still living with his mother and we saw for ourselves that it wasn't exactly in luxury, there. Nothing is known about any Brets/Brassel contact in the past. They didn't know each other before Brassel sought out Brets for the alleged break-in at Bunsum. Thus we must see all this in the light of preparation for murder. The real motive is not connected to any of it. It's something that happened before."

They were stopped in front of a red light, so Vledder darted a quick glance aside, his face beaming.

"Excellent, really excellent," he cried enthusiastically. Neither man noticed that he was using one of DeKok's stock phrases. "You have something there. Nobody has to teach you how to suck eggs. Nossir, a clear, concise explanation. Completely logical." He grinned while engaging the clutch in response to the green light. "Your performance at the Brassels was also a classic, by the way. That little white lie about not finding the note shook him to the core."

DeKok smiled at the memory.

"Yes," he admitted, "our Pierre lost his cool there for a while. In a way I was a bit surprised. I would have thought that his position was a lot stronger."

"What do you mean?"

DeKok sighed.

"I thought he was less vulnerable."

Vledder nodded.

"What do you think, will we be able to charge him with something, when the time comes?"

"I hope not."

"What!?"

DeKok shook his head.

"No, really," he said, his face serious. "I mean it. I hope we will never have to charge him with any specific crime. I wouldn't like that at all, at all. I would sincerely regret it. I find him a thoroughly sympathetic man."

It was a good thing they were in the city, partially sheltered from the gale force weather. Vledder almost lost control of the car in utter surprise.

"Brassel," he chided, "a sympathetic guy? That arrogant, supercilious gentleman, who is trying his best to make us look ridiculous? You're crazy. If his little game ever becomes common knowledge, you can kiss your reputation goodbye."

DeKok shrugged his shoulders.

"Ach," he responded with a wan smile, "my reputation can stand the occasional mud slinging. That's the least of my worries, it's not all that important."

He rubbed his face with both hands.

"You see, I actually pitied Brassel tonight. I watched him very carefully. There was more fear than bluster. The apparently oh so superior Mr. Brassel is scared stiff that something may have gone wrong. He's not sure of himself. Despite his careful preparations, his studies of the relevant jurisprudence, he's afraid we can charge him with something. Just think about his vehement behavior when I spoke of complicity."

Vledder nodded.

"That's true. But I don't think that's a reason to think he's sympathetic."

He guided the battered VW around the monument on the Dam and aimed it into the Warmoes Street. He stopped in front of the entrance to the station house.

The desk sergeant gave them a long suffering look when Vledder and DeKok appeared in his line of sight.

"Dammit," he called, "where *were* you two?"

DeKok looked at him. His eyes questioned the speaker.

"What's up, then?"

"I tried to reach you everywhere. Your car radio must be on the blink again, or did you turn it off? Anyway, I've had a guy here for the last few hours and I don't know what to do with him."

"What guy?"

"One Freddy Blaken. He came in to give himself up."

* * *

DeKok's glance took in the young man. Then he pointed at a chair next to his desk.

"Won't you sit down?" he invited. "To what do we owe the pleasure of your visit?"

Freddy Blaken looked suspiciously at the gray sleuth.

"Pleasure? Ain't I wanted?"

DeKok gave him a friendly grin.

"In a way, but I just want to chat with you for a while. For instance, about your friend Jan Brets and his untimely demise. You apparently had no time for us, this afternoon. You seemed rushed."

The young man nodded slowly.

"I shouldn't have run," he sighed. It sounded sincere. "That was dumb. Real dumb. I figured that out later. That's why I came to give myself up. I'm trying to make up for the bad impression you might have about me. I didn't kill Jan Brets."

DeKok grimaced, a look of utter astonishment on his face.

"But didn't you say, in the presence of witnesses, I might add, that you were going to bash in his skull?"

Freddy lowered his head and nodded.

"Yes, I did," he admitted tonelessly, "But ..."

"Well," interrupted DeKok, "that same day, only a few hours later, Brets was killed, murdered. Somebody had bashed in his skull. A remarkable coincidence, don't you think?"

Blaken shook his head.

"I didn't do it," he said simply.

DeKok ignored the remark.

"Ach," he said, gesturing grandly, "it's fairy tale time, is it? Well, I have a number of coincidences. Let me enumerate."

Blaken jumped out of his chair.

"No," he cried emphatically, "I didn't do it."

DeKok placed a surprisingly strong hand on the shoulder of the young man and gently, but irresistibly, forced him back on the chair.

"You will listen," he said severely, "to what I have to say, Mr. Blaken, or don't you want to know why I could have had you arrested this afternoon, when you took off in such a hurry?"

The young man swallowed. His adam's apple bobbed up and down.

"Go ahead," he said softly. "Please," he added as an afterthought.

DeKok rubbed his hands through his hair, as if to gather his thoughts. Vledder was sometimes amused, but usually a bit irritated with those theatricals.

"There were, Mr. Blaken, only a few people who knew that Jan Brets was staying at the Greenland Arms. You were one of the few. You were a member of the so-called syndicate. You knew that Brets was in Amsterdam to prepare the ground, so to speak. Therefore you knew where to reach him in your murderous fury." He made a vague gesture while he let the words sink in. Then he added: "That doesn't bode well for you, when taken into context with your earlier statements, about bashing skulls and so on. Also, you had a motive."

The young man looked up, shocked and scared.

"Motive?"

DeKok nodded with special emphasis.

"Jealousy. You were jealous of Brets because of the interest he had in Cynthia. Jealousy, Mr. Blaken, is a powerful motive for murder." He paused. "And another thing, young sir, the body of Brets had been placed in a position that closely resembled a harlequin, and you were the only one to have ever called him a clown and a joker." DeKok pushed his lower lip forward. "What do you think?" he asked with sarcasm. "With that sort of evidence, what would your chances be in front of a judge?"

Again Blaken shook his head vigorously.

"I didn't do it," he exclaimed. "It's all false, false, false."

DeKok sighed.

"How long have you known Pierre Brassel?"

"Brassel?"

"Yes."

"I don't know him."

DeKok looked at him intently. A dangerous fire sparkled in the back of his eyes.

"You must know him."

Blaken hid his face in his hands.

"I don't know him. I don't know him." There was despair in the voice.

"Didn't Brets introduce you?"

"No, I never met Brassel. Jan told me about him. That's true. He was supposed to be the man behind the scenes, the organizer, the tipster."

DeKok nodded.

"When was 'Operation Harlequin' scheduled for execution?"

Blaken looked at him with a stupid look on his face.

"Operation Harlequin?"

"Yes."

"I, ... eh, ... I don't know. I've never heard of no Operation Harlequin."

DeKok's eyebrows started one of their fantastic dances. Lightly they seemed to trip around his forehead, swaying to some unheard music. Despite his predicament, Blaken seemed momentarily fascinated. Vledder frowned in a subconscious effort to duplicate the feat.

"Then," cried DeKok in exasperation, "what in blazes did Brassel need *you* for?"

"Because of my connections. In case there was anything to sell. I have relations, relations that buy things and ask no questions. Jan knew that. I've helped him out, sometimes, with excess inventory." He looked at DeKok with the expression of a faithful dog. "You see, I'm not the curious type. Well, in the past ... yes. But I stopped being curious. I never ask things. If you're in the fencing business, you're better off if your left hand doesn't know what your right hand is doing. Believe me, the less I know, the less I will tell. It's safer, too."

DeKok smiled.

"But," he tried, "Jan Brets visited you regularly."

Freddy displayed a sad grin.

"He didn't come to see me. Not for business, that is. He came for Cynthia. The bastard. He *knew* we'd been engaged for two years and were planning to get married." He paused, shrugged his shoulders. "You shouldn't wish anybody dead, not even your worst enemy. But Jan Brets deserved it. He was asking for it. I don't know who did him in, finally. I swear I don't know. But it had to happen, sooner or later."

DeKok nodded. Then he rose from his chair and walked over to the peg in the wall where he usually hung his raincoat.

"Come on," he tossed over his shoulder, "let's go."

Vledder looked at him in surprise.

"*We* go?" He glanced at Freddy.

DeKok nodded.

"Put on your coat and hold on to Freddy."

They left the detective room and walked down the long, old fashioned corridor to the stairs. They greeted the desk sergeant on the way out and before long they were on the Damrak, the widest street in Amsterdam. The Damrak connects the Dam Square, so beloved by transients today and hippies and flower children in the past, to the Station Square, in front of the Central Railroad Station. In the middle of the deserted street DeKok halted.

"Take Freddy to Hotel Dupont," he ordered, "and tell the owner it's all right."

"What about you?"

DeKok gave him a tired smile.

"I'm going home. I'll walk. I need the fresh air."

He waved in farewell and disappeared in the rain.

Vledder and Blaken stared after him.

They saw him waddle along the pavement on the other side of the street, his raincoat tight around his large body, his little felt hat tipped far forward. He looked like a late drunk who had been refused a last drink in the bar from which he had been ejected.

He did not turn around.

16

DeKok paced angrily up and down the large detective room. He was in a foul mood. His face looked like a thundercloud. It was nine o'clock and there was no coffee. The culprit was the new, very young detective Bonmeyer. According to the duty roster he was supposed to have taken care of the coffee this morning. But a report of a burglary and the interrogation of a woman had seemed more important to the inexperienced detective. In DeKok's eyes this was simply unpardonable. Nothing could be more important than coffee, especially in the morning. That is why he read poor Bonmeyer the riot act in the choicest possible terms. He had a lot to learn, according to DeKok, especially the making of coffee at the right time, no matter what else was happening. Even if the Royal Palace was burning down, he, DeKok, would still expect coffee to be ready.

Right in the middle of another thundering sentence, wherein he repeated his dissatisfaction with the state of affairs, the phone rang. With a wild gesture DeKok grabbed the telephone and yelled that the other party had reached the police.

His tone changed almost immediately when he learned who was at the other end of the line.

"Good morning, Mrs. Brassel, what can I do for you? ... An appointment? But, of course ... This morning, at ten? Most certainly, but where? Here? ... Ah, rather not at the station, I understand, so where do you suggest? ... What's that you said? ... Yes, the restaurant in the Amstel Station? Yes, I know where that is, no problem ... Until then, good day, Mrs. Brassel."

Gently he replaced the receiver and scratched his neck. What did handsome Mrs. Brassel want? Why a meeting on neutral grounds? A commuter railroad station in the suburbs was not the ideal place for an assignation. He immediately rejected the possibility that she had fallen head-over-heels in love with him. That was simply too absurd. Even his own wife, a model of indulgence, had taken years to get used to his good-natured boxer face. No, he reflected with a sigh, it would be business, just business. Anyway, they would have fresh coffee in the restaurant.

He closed the drawer of his desk, threw one more devastating look in the direction of the hapless Bonmeyer, pulled on his coat and left the room in a sulky mood.

Downstairs he met the old Commissaris as he entered the station. DeKok quickly pulled up the collar of his coat in a forlorn attempt to hide and tried to escape via the rear entrance. He was doomed to failure.

"DeKok!"

Slowly DeKok turned around, forced a friendly grin on his face and approached his chief reluctantly.

"Good morning, sir."

The Commissaris lifted his hat.

"Good morning, DeKok," he said cheerfully, "come with me a moment, would you?"

DeKok rubbed his chin.

"I ... eh, ... I have an appointment at ten," he tried.

The commissars looked at his watch.

"Oh," he laughed, "plenty of time."

He climbed the stairs with remarkable agility for a man of his advanced years. DeKok followed him a little slower.

The Commissaris threw his briefcase on a table. Still with his coat on, he sat down behind the desk and stretched an arm toward DeKok.

"Give me your report," he said. His tone was serious. "We'll have time to go over it together."

DeKok swallowed.

"Report? What report?"

The Commissaris frowned.

"I do believe," he said, irritation in his voice, "that we had agreed. You, or young Vledder, would give me a detailed report regarding the happenings at the Greenland Arms."

DeKok bowed his head.

"That's true," he said with well-feigned deference. "You're right. But I don't have it yet. There's been no time. Anyway, there are no details to report. Jan Brets was knocked down with a reinforced hockey stick. That was all in the preliminary report that Vledder and I wrote." He shrugged his shoulders. "There's little to add to that," he concluded.

Angrily, the Commissaris rose from his chair.

"I want a *detailed* report."

DeKok made an apologetic gesture.

"I don't have it."

"Then you prepare it, at once!"

"I have an appointment."

The Commissaris was getting red in the face.

"I want," he yelled, furious, "I want a detailed report *today*! You understand? I want a detailed report about the Brets case, no matter how. Today! From you!"

161

DeKok was already in a foul mood because of the coffee. With difficulty he suppressed a number of less suitable observations. Instead he bit his lip, sighed deeply and asked with mocking politeness if the Commissaris had any other orders.

Yes, the Commissaris did. It seemed that the management of the Greenland Arms had asked repeatedly when the seals of Room 21 could be removed. It had been almost two days. They were losing money.

DeKok could not contain himself any longer.

"Dammit," he exploded, "altogether it's been less than forty eight hours since Jan Brets was murdered and already they're whining about a sealed room and my boss is whining about a report. I'm surprised no questions have yet been asked in Parliament!"

The Commissaris roared a single word:

"OUT!!!"

DeKok left.

* * *

The coffee in the small restaurant of the Amstel Station went a long way to reconciling him with his fate. The day had started badly, he thought. If it continued that way, this could be one of those days . . . Anyway, he thought philosophically, that's the life of a cop. Up and down, you never knew what was going to happen next.

He thought about the interview with his chief. A detailed report. He grinned to himself. You did not solve murders by writing reports. It only wasted a lot of time. The Commissaris should know that. He ordered a second cup of coffee and waited resignedly for the appearance of Brassel's wife. He pushed his chair a little back and looked around.

He had picked a strategic position. He could overlook the entire room from this spot. There were but a few people. Mostly men, probably sales people, to judge from the sample cases. Most tables were unused.

* * *

Mrs. Brassel was reasonably prompt. It was just a few minutes past ten when she entered the restaurant; an exceptionally striking, handsome woman with noticeable blonde hair, dressed in a black astrakhan coat. Her appearance drew immediate attention from the few people in the restaurant. It was if a sudden wind blew through the room. It was accompanied by an undefinable rustling.

Calmly she looked around the room and when she spotted him, she approached him resolutely with firm, long strides. There was a determined set to her mouth.

DeKok admired the feline suppleness of her body and the undeniable grace with which she moved. She reminds me of a panther, he thought, with barely withdrawn claws.

DeKok was convinced that he was looking at the woman with the German accent who had tried to reach Jan Brets shortly before his death. Had she intended to warn him. What did she know?

Slowly he stood up.

"Good morning, Mrs. Brassel."

"Good morning, Inspector."

He helped take her coat off and held her chair with old-world gallantry. A sweet scent of perfume rose from her hair.

"Coffee?"

"Please."

DeKok ordered from the approaching waiter. It was his third cup, but who was counting? Smiling, he sat down across from her and unashamedly looked intently at her for a long time. She withstood his scrutiny with proud indifference.

"You're an extremely handsome woman," he said after a while. "Yes, indeed, extremely handsome." It sounded official, no more than the establishment of fact. He continued: "It seems to be the fate of beautiful women to get into trouble. I sometimes wonder, is that a result of their beauty, or is it something else?"

She smiled.

"I wouldn't worry about it."

The waiter arrived with the coffee.

Both remained silent. DeKok stirred his coffee thoughtfully and stared at her right hand on the table top. The hand shook a little.

"I take it," he said finally, in his most unconcerned tone of voice, "that your husband sent you?"

"No!"

It sounded so sharp that DeKok was forced to look at her.

"No," she repeated, "I come of my own accord. My husband knows nothing about this. He's in the office. I found a baby sitter for the kids." She sighed deeply. "But I cannot stay long."

DeKok nodded understanding.

"Well," he said with an inviting gesture, "the floor is yours. I'm listening."

She nervously crushed an empty sugar wrapper. A nervous tic trembled at the corners of her full, sensuous lips.

"Well," urged DeKok, "you certainly didn't ask to meet me because of my irresistible charm."

164

She gave him a sweet smile. Her hand reached across the table. The tips of her fingers barely touched his arm. The touch, however slight, gave DeKok a warm feeling. It made his skin tingle.

"You're a friendly person," she said softly.

"I don't rightly know," he answered sadly, "if I should consider that a compliment. I mean, from the mouth of a beautiful young woman."

She looked at him with incomprehension.

DeKok pursed his lips and shook his head.

"Pay no attention to me," he said with a solemn voice. "Today seems to be shaping up as one of those days when everything goes wrong. You better tell me what I can do for you."

"I'm worried."

"About your husband?"

She nodded.

"Yes, about my husband. You see, despite all his careful preparations and precisely worked out plans, I'm afraid that something will go wrong."

"Wrong with what?"

She lowered her head and did not answer.

"With what, Mrs. Brassel? What could go wrong with what?"

She gave him a cheerless look.

"I'm sorry, Mr. DeKok. Believe me, I'm really sorry. I wish I could be more specific. It would put my mind more at ease. But I really cannot tell you."

DeKok narrowed his eyes.

"Then why did you ask to meet me?" He sounded annoyed. "Why did you come here? If you cannot be open with me, this meeting serves no useful purpose."

He rose as if to leave. She immediately placed a restraining hand on his sleeve.

"Please, sit down," she begged. "I want to ask you something. I have a request."

"A request?"

"Yes."

DeKok gestured expansively.

"Go on, then," he encouraged, "I can never deny the requests of beautiful women."

A wan smile flitted over her face.

"I," she sighed, "don't ask much."

"Well, I'm listening."

She looked at him. Her eyes were beseeching.

"When you go home tonight, Mr. DeKok," she whispered, "you will find an invitation for a rummage sale in Oldwater, near where we live."

"Yes."

She moved a blonde strand away from her face.

"I urge you most earnestly to accept the invitation, Mr. DeKok. You and your wife should come to the sale."

DeKok shrugged his shoulders in a careless movement.

"Why?"

She gave him a penetrating look.

"I already told you, my husband knows nothing about this. I do this on my own. I know the invitation has been sent. I also know why. My husband hopes you'll come. He is, however, of the opinion that your presence isn't strictly necessary. He expects that there will be enough people at the gathering who will recognize us. Perhaps he's right. But I'm afraid, Mr. DeKok, I'm afraid. Most people have a poor memory for faces. Not you, Mr. DeKok, not you. You're a trained policeman, used to observing, used to remembering salient facts. That's why, you see, I want you to be there."

She spoke in a compelling voice, convincingly, with barely controlled emotions.

"I have two small children, Mr. DeKok, it doesn't bear thinking about that ..."

" ... that Pierre," completed DeKok, "should go to jail."

She nodded slowly, reluctantly.

"You understand."

DeKok picked up his cup and slowly drained the last of his coffee. Her words echoed in his head, resonating back and forth on the inside of his skull. After a while he replaced the empty cup and rubbed his chin in a pensive manner.

"You know the plans?"

"Yes."

"And you were the woman who called Brets at the Greenland Arms, shortly after eight?"

She nodded almost imperceptibly.

"Why?"

She did not answer.

DeKok pressed his lips together.

"Then I will tell you," he spoke bitterly. "You wanted to soothe your conscience with a telephone call. A miserable attempt. You *knew* that eight o'clock would be too late."

Her eyes spat fire.

"I couldn't get through," she hissed.

"Otherwise you would have told Brets what was about to happen?"

She bent her head and remained silent. Her cheeks trembled, as if she was about to cry.

DeKok faced a dilemma. He did not know what to do next. He rubbed his lips with the back of his hand and looked at the woman across the table. How far could he go? How far *dared* he go? How far could he go and still live with himself?

"Mrs. Brassel," he said, hesitating about the choice of words. "I, . . . eh, could interrogate you officially, right here, in the restaurant. I'm sure I could mislead you and make you admit things you would rather keep a secret. Believe me, I know all the tricks. Then I could use your answers for my own purposes. The answers could lead me to other sources, or conclusions, which I could use against your husband."

He paused and rested his elbows on the table.

"I could do all that, but I won't."

He looked at her, his head cocked to one side.

"But I do have *one* question . . ."

"Yes."

"Who will be killed tonight?"

Mrs. Brassel paled. Her mouth fell open and she looked at him with wide, frightened eyes. She was stunned.

"Who," repeated DeKok, "will be killed tonight?"

A shrill, incoherent sound escaped her lips.

Then she recovered. Abruptly she stood up, grabbed her coat and ran for the exit. She did not take the time to put her coat on. She fled, as if pursued by all the devils from hell.

DeKok watched her leave unemotionally. Calmly he remained seated, his broad face an expressionless mask.

The waiter approached.

"The lady was in a hurry," he concluded.

DeKok nodded and ordered his fourth cup of coffee.

17

With his trouser legs rolled up to his knees, DeKok resembled an old fisherman from times gone by. But he was home, his painful feet in a tub of hot water with baking soda. He cursed. He cursed everything. He cursed his narrow shoes and the formal, black suit he had worn for the funeral of Jan Brets, earlier that day. He cursed Ma Brets who had stained his shirt with her tears and running mascara. He cursed Cynthia Worden who had appeared at the funeral dressed like a silly schoolgirl and who had behaved accordingly. And above all, he cursed himself, for staying so long in Utrecht, aimlessly strolling through the unfamiliar streets of the for him so strange city, until his painful feet had finally forced him to sit down at the edge of the pavement to untie his shoelaces.

Except for the funeral, he had no business in Utrecht at all, he now understood. Every time he ignored the warning of his feet, things would go wrong. The solution to the riddle was not to be found in Utrecht. Jan Brets had lived there, but that was all.

His wife approached with a fresh kettle of hot water.

"You want a little more hot water?"

DeKok lifted his dripping feet and looked at the stream of hot water with suspicious hawk's eyes.

"All right, already," he cried anxiously, "not so much. You want to burn me? I'm not a lobster!"

His wife laughed and felt the temperature of the water with concerned concentration.

"Just right, like this."

DeKok carefully lowered his legs until his feet touched the water. Starting with the toes he slowly submerged his feet. After a painful grimace, a comfortable, idiotic smile appeared on his face.

His faithful dog, who had watched his master from a hiding spot in the corner of the room while the cursing was going on, carefully crept closer. DeKok petted the dog and gave his wife a friendly grin. Slowly the pain left his feet.

"Did you," he asked pleasantly, "receive an invitation this morning for some kind of rummage sale?"

She looked surprised.

"How did you know?"

DeKok laughed mysteriously.

"Let me see it, please."

She walked over tho the small desk in the corner of the comfortable room and returned with the card.

"Here you are."

DeKok accepted the card from her and looked it all over. It was a simple invitation to a rummage sale, there would be dancing afterward. The event was to be held in the building of the YMCA by the organization 'Oldwater Forwards!' The proceeds were to benefit several Boy Scout groups in the little river town.

"This came by mail?"

His wife shook her head.

"It was delivered."

"How delivered?"

"A slender young man, about thirty." She pointed at a vase filled with tulips on the sideboard. "With flowers and a recipe."

DeKok grinned.

"Cake recipe?"

His wife sat down.

"Yes, you knew? A complicated recipe."

DeKok smiled at the questioning face of his wife.

"Try it sometimes," he said, "success assured."

She looked at him searchingly.

"Jurriaan," she said in a compelling voice, "what does it mean?"

DeKok's wife was the only one who sometimes called him by his first name. It was an unusual name, even in Holland. It came from one of the small islands in the Zuyder Zee. The island had long since become a part of the mainland as a result of the Dutch penchant for creating their own living space. In this case they had "simply" built a dike around large parts of the Zuyder Zee, pumped the water out and built farms on what had once been the bottom of the sea. DeKok's island was now a rather large hill in the middle of corn fields. The harbor, where his father's fishing boat had been moored, was now a museum.

"Jurriaan," she repeated, "tell me about it."

"What?"

"Who was the young man? Why the flowers and the recipe? What about the invitation?"

DeKok raised both arms in the air.

"Stop," he protested. "Not all at once. I don't have all the answers. Not yet. The good looking young man must have been Pierre Brassel. The recipe is from his very charming wife and as for the invitation, we accept."

171

His wife did not take her eyes off him.

"Tonight," mocked DeKok, "we will mingle with the upper crust of Oldwater in order to admire and promote the attempts to improve the usage of leisure hours by the Oldwater youth. We will cheerfully buy a few white elephants, try our luck at Bingo and trip the light fantastic until the early hours of the morning."

Mrs. DeKok listened more to the tone, than to the content of his words. Something bothered her. Slowly she rose from her chair and stood behind him. With a gentle caress she placed her hand on his bristly gray hair.

"DeKok . . ."

"Yes."

"Why are we accepting the invitation?"

DeKok wriggled his toes in the tub of soda water, creating tiny wavelets.

"Ach," he said, ducking the question, "a rummage sale, a dance, it seems like fun."

She smiled behind his back.

"Funny," she remarked, "I never knew you cared so much for village life."

DeKok sighed deeply.

"Now the serpent," he cited the Bible, *"was more subtil than any beast of the field . . ."*

She played her fingers through his hair.

"DeKok . . . ," her voice was insistent, "what's the reason for the invitation?"

He turned abruptly so that the water spilled from the tub.

"Murder," he said roughly. "Now give me the towel."

* * *

The YMCA building, near the center of Oldwater, across from the bus stop in front of the Town Hall, was little more than a small auditorium, a smaller stage, a minuscule lobby and, off to one side, a small gym.

But it was pleasantly crowded.

The farmers from around the village, the civil servants and business people of the bedroom community, the shopkeepers in the small town, all had responded to the invitation. They walked around and looked at the offerings. A small combo was setting up on the tiny stage. Middle aged ladies with permanently waved hair were everywhere, organizing, cajoling, supervising. They were the driving force behind the organization "Oldwater Forwards!" They sold tickets for door prizes, ran the bingo game and were in charge of the few stalls, where one could throw balls at a stack of tin cans, or darts for prizes. One sharp eyed old lady kept a close watch on the young girl in the Kissing Booth.

DeKok participated in everything except, maybe in deference to his wife, or the sharp eyed old lady, the Kissing Booth.

He threw balls and missed, he dunked his heavy body into a barrel filled with a lot of sawdust and a few meaningless prizes, threw darts and missed and had his fortune told by the "Gypsy" fortuneteller, who was actually the wife of the local minister. She promised him a long life. "How long?" asked DeKok. The minister's wife smiled sweetly. "For terms of more than a hundred years," she joked, "I refer you to my husband." DeKok laughed heartily. Fine people, he thought, here in Oldwater. What a shindig to organize this late in the Century. It took him back to his youth.

But he did not forget to keep a weather eye open for Brassel. Brassel had not yet arrived. DeKok consulted his watch. It was a little after eight. He was surprised. According to his calculations, Brassel should have been present already. Unless, he reflected, unless another time had been picked.

He nudged his wife.

"Do you see your young man anywhere?" he asked.

She stood on her toes and looked around.

"No, I don't see him. Is he supposed to be here?"

DeKok nodded.

"If I'm right, he's bound to show up. He needs us."

"For murder?"

DeKok grinned.

"You could say that."

He took his wife by the arm and together they pushed their way to the entrance.

"Are we leaving?"

"No, no, we're staying close. I want to know when he shows up."

They had almost reached the door when Brassel appeared.

DeKok withdrew slightly. He saw Brassel's eyes search the room. He was followed by his wife holding six-year old Ingrid by the hand. His wife, too, looked nervous. She pulled the child closer to her. It was an impatient movement.

DeKok pressed himself forward in the crowd. He observed how Brassel's glance caught sight of him. He shaped his face into an expression of delighted surprise.

Brassel motioned to his wife. With little Ingrid between them, they approached.

The usual formalities followed.

"I see," said Brassel, after everybody had met each other, "that you have accepted the invitation."

DeKok feigned a puzzled look. His wife intervened tactfully.

"This is the young man," she said cheerfully, "who delivered the invitation this morning."

"Oh," exclaimed DeKok. His sudden understanding was worthy of an Academy Award. "So, the invitation was *your* idea?"

Brassel laughed.

"Yes," he admitted, "or rather, it was my wife's idea. At first it was not part of the plan."

The two women quickly found enough common interests. Together they walked off in the direction of the "bargain" tables. DeKok had taken little Ingrid by the hand. With Brassel and the little girl between them, they followed the women.

The rummage sale was in full swing. There were sales of locally produced embroidery, knitwear and handicrafts of surprising, sometimes exquisite quality.

"You were," DeKok said nonchalantly, "a few minutes late."

Brassel nodded.

"We hadn't planned to bring Ingrid," he explained, "but she woke at the last minute as we were ready to leave, coats on. She knew immediately that we were going out and there was no way she was going to stay home without us. There was no other choice, we had to take her with us. Then we first had to get her dressed. It all took time."

DeKok laughed.

"Yes," he grinned, "the best laid plans of man and mice . . ."

Meanwhile he came closer to Brassel.

"Who," he whispered, *"is getting killed tonight?"*

Brassel looked shocked.

"I-I . . . , eh, I d-don't understand you," he stuttered.

DeKok's eyebrows moved. Several people looked suddenly fascinated, but when the eyebrows quickly resumed their normal appearance, they obviously thought they had been mistaken.

"Ach, come on, Brassel," DeKok's tone was full of reproach. "Of course you understand me. It's silly to deny it. My wife and I and all visitors here tonight have but one purpose: to serve as your alibi. And the simple fact that you seem to need an alibi, points to another murder."

Brassel reacted strongly.

"What are you saying?" He hissed the question. "Are you implying that I'm only here because I need an alibi? Who says I need an alibi?"

DeKok grinned broadly

"I do."

In passing he took a local beauty by the arm. The girl was selling carnations from a large wicker basket. She was indeed a good looking girl of about twenty years. Healthy, with long blond pigtails, soulful eyes and a sweet mouth.

"What's your name?" asked DeKok.

"Francine," answered the girl.

"What else?"

"Francine Brakel."

DeKok smiled in a friendly way.

"Nice name." He pointed at Brassel.

"This gentleman wants to buy one of your carnations. But please pick a nice one. One that goes well with his handsome face."

He took the flower girl by an arm and clicked his tongue.

"Have you noticed," he joked, "How handsome this gentleman is? A regular Apollo!" He grinned. "Oh, well," he continued, "perhaps not an Adonis, but in any case a man you will remember all your life. The sort of man you dream about."

The girl looked at Brassel's face and giggled. Still giggling she pinned a carnation to his lapel. Brassel just stood there, obviously embarrassed. He quickly pulled some money out of his pocket and paid with a sour face.

From across the girl's shoulder, DeKok looked at him derisively. He enjoyed the moment. After the beauty and her basket had disappeared he said mockingly:

"You see, Brassel, that's how you create alibis. You don't need a cop for that. I thought I'd give you a demonstration, because I don't feel much like being invited the next time you plan a murder."

He shook his head and spread his arms wide.

"But I do wonder how long you intend to keep it up. Really, seriously, Brassel, how many more murders are on the agenda?"

Brassel faced him fully, abruptly. His eyes glowed angrily.

"What do you think I am?" His tone was indignant, offended. "I'm not an animal, not a maniac."

DeKok shrugged his shoulders in manner meant to be irritating.

"How would I know? I've seen no psychiatric evaluation of you. What guarantees me that you're not an antisocial deviate, bent on destruction? Perhaps you have an irresistible urge to wipe out entire communities. At first glance, I'll admit, you look quite normal."

The laconic, calm, almost careless conversational tone of DeKok did have the intended effect on Brassel. He was visibly upset. An excited blush spread over his face.

"I'm not crazy!"

He yelled so loud that people turned their heads and stared. Mrs. Brassel, too, turned around. In the blink of an eye she correctly appraised her husband's loss of self-control. She stopped and came closer.

"What's the matter, Pierre," she asked, concerned. "Who says you're crazy?"

Brassel did not answer.

She looked at DeKok. There was an icy, disapproving look in her eyes. And just a hint of hate.

DeKok grinned and little Ingrid, all but forgotten, suddenly cried:

"*Hampelmann!*"

The word exploded.

A drum roll, a cannon shot, nothing could have upset the Brassels more on this festive evening than the single word "Hampelmann" from the innocent mouth of little Ingrid.

The Brassels seemed to freeze in their tracks.

DeKok watched with calm fascination. He registered what he saw. That was all. He saw the shocked faces of the couple and then, as if in slow motion, he felt how Ingrid's hand was being pulled from his own, large hand. He watched as Mrs. Brassel took the little girl protectively under her wing. He felt the nervous tension, but did not understand it.

Again the little girl repeated the word "Hampelmann" and pointed upward.

Somewhere in the maelstrom of his memories, DeKok searched for a handhold, a sense of reality. He often prided himself on his inability to think like a computer, to think in a straight line. He knew his thought processes were not always logical, they seemed to jump from one subject to another and would reach conclusions that were as much the result of instinct and intuition, as well as reason, backed by an enormous amount of experience. With his eyes he followed the outstretched finger of the little girl. Then, in a sudden flash of recognition, a clear spark of association, all veils fell away and he suddenly saw the various bits and pieces of information fall into place. Suddenly he understood the how and the why of the murders.

On an improvised stall he saw wooden marionettes with tall dunce caps. They were hand painted. The bodies, arms and legs in black and white diamonds. The noses were bright red and little yellow suns with minuscule rays were painted on the cheeks. Small strings hung down from the dolls. When the strings were pulled, the arms and legs would move in rhythmic unison. DeKok selected the best looking harlequin.

He squatted down and motioned. Mrs. Brassel could not hold little Ingrid. The little girl struggled free and ran excitedly toward DeKok. Her eyes were bright with joy.

A friendly grin appeared on DeKok's face.

"Hier mein Kind," he said in his best German, *"Hier hast du deinen Hampelmann."**

---

* "Here, my child, here is your harlequin."

18

Inspector DeKok rose slowly from his squatting position. The friendly and indulgent expression on his face, that had been there while he gave Ingrid her wooden harlequin, had disappeared. His usually good-natured, craggy face was hard, almost grim.

He walked toward Brassel, his mouth compressed into a straight line, his heavy torso under a slight incline. His posture was so threatening that Brassel stepped back, farther, and farther.

DeKok walked on, slowly, but inexorably. It looked as if nothing could stop him, an irresistible force of nature. Pierre Brassel fled, evaded until he could go no further. He ran backwards into a group of bantering farmers. Only when he tried to escape again, did DeKok grab him. He placed his large, hairy hand on Brassel's chest and bunched the man's shirt into his fist.

"Who?"

Pierre Brassel panted heavily, but did not answer. His nostrils quivered and there was fear in his eyes. Nervous tics ran along his cheeks.

"Who?"

Brassel remained silent.

DeKok tensed his arm and pulled him closer. Brassel's face was right in front of his own. The material of the shirt creaked under the strain.

"Who!?" roared DeKok.

The raw bellow bounced against the walls and shocked several visitors. All interest in charity disappeared suddenly. A crowd gathered around Brassel and DeKok. Neither bingo, nor the fortune-telling minister's wife could compete with the sight of the two men. The hopeful expectation of a good fight held the onlookers spellbound.

Upset by the unexpected and unwanted commotion, a few of the elderly ladies rushed to the scene. Determined and with the tenacity of dowagers on the rampage they tried to separate the two men. They were doomed to failure. DeKok did not let go.

"Who?" he roared again. "Perhaps I can still prevent it!" He shook the younger man so powerfully that he actually lifted him off his feet. His rage was monumental. "Damn you, creep," he hissed, "speak up!"

Brassel hung his head.

"Too late," he said softly, "too late."

DeKok released him. He took his wife by the arm and left the YMCA building with head held high.

"I'll never again go out with you. Never again. As long as you don't know how to behave, I won't be seen in public with you."

Mrs. DeKok was angry, shocked and obstinate. Her bosom rose and fell with sheer indignation. Her face was red.

"Those Brassels ... such nice people, and you attack that poor man ... like a ... like a *street fighter*! How dare you!? It's all because of the job. I know, you're a cop. But that's no reason to forget your manners. It's ... it's ... *immoral!*"

DeKok gripped the steering wheel of his old car a little tighter and sighed.

"I'm sorry, darling," he apologized. "Really, I'm truly sorry." He looked crestfallen. "But you see, I *had* to try. There was a small chance. If Pierre had spoken ..." He paused. "It would have been so much easier and perhaps I would have been able to save a life." He swallowed. "Otherwise I would never have done it. You believe me, don't you? You know how I am, I don't like force."

She looked at him from the side and studied the expression on his face.

"I don't always know for sure," she said hesitantly, "when you work your police tricks on me, I'm lost, sometimes." She smiled suddenly. "I don't understand a thing about the invitation to the bazaar. What was it all about?"

DeKok shook his head.

"You don't have to understand it," he smiled in response. "I'll explain it all to you, later. For now, it's still a bit complicated and it would take too long."

She sighed.

"But it's about murder, isn't it? That's what you said this afternoon."

"Yes, yes," he said, "it's about murder all right, or rather, about *two* murders."

"Two?"

DeKok nodded.

"Look," he explained patiently, "while we were enjoying the rummage sale with the Brassels, a second murder was being committed. And both of them knew it. They knew it was going to happen."

"Where?"

DeKok shrugged his shoulders.

"I don't know."

"Who's being murdered?"

DeKok shook his head sadly.

"That too, I don't know."

She laughed with just a tiny hint of contempt.

"What *do* you know?"

DeKok let the car slow down slightly and searched for a stick of chewing gum. His face was worried.

"Listen," he said in a hopeless tone of voice, "I know enough, believe me. I know enough to bring this case to a conclusion. Pierre Brassel understood that, tonight. I had hoped that he would lift the veil of mystery now that he knew, at least understood, that I had seen through him. But he did not. He kept his mouth tightly shut. I wonder why. It seems so senseless."

His wife scooted a little closer to him and placed a familiar hand on his knee. Her anger about his behavior seemed to have dissipated.

"Perhaps," she said sweetly, "perhaps you don't know enough yet. It could be that Pierre has some more surprises for you."

DeKok sighed.

"Perhaps. But now I know the 'why' of the Brets murder. And although I don't know the name offhand, I do know who was killed tonight."

His wife looked at him with frightened eyes.

"But ... , b-but," she stammered, "if you knew that ahead of time, why did you let it happen?"

DeKok pressed his lips together.

"I let nobody be murdered," he said sharply, much sharper than he had intended. "I didn't know it ahead of time. I only started to understand tonight. Not before. Call it stupidity, lack of insight." He shrugged his shoulders. "I don't care what you call it, but not until tonight did I see the solution. It's positively shameful that a six-year old had to point the way, give me the clue."

"Clue?"

DeKok grinned, nodding his head.

"Hampelmann."

* * *

DeKok lounged lazily behind his desk in the aged, renowned, infamous police station at the Warmoes Street in Amsterdam. The reports about Jan Brets were in front of him, on his desk. DeKok had gone home and dragged the old documents, arrest reports, dispositions, depositions and sentencing decrees to the office. Again he had gone over them all, much more quickly than before, because he knew what he was looking for.

Then he had gone to the house of Celine, Dick Vledder's fiancee and announced that Vledder had to report to the office immediately and at once.

The attractive Celine had protested vehemently, had murmured things about slave drivers and, if looks could have killed, the gray sleuth would have been reduced to burning embers on the spot. But Vledder, reluctantly, stepped into the car and that was what DeKok wanted.

"I had just got here," growled Vledder. "I haven't seen her all week. So what's up? What's so all-fired important? You could have let me be, for one night. Dammit, I have a right to . . ."

DeKok waited patiently until the torrent of words had dried up. He understood his young partner, but he needed him.

"How can we find Renard Kamperman?"

"What!?"

"How can we find Renard Kamperman?" repeated DeKok.

Vledder looked at him from the side, his mouth open, surprise in his eyes.

"Who is Renard Kamperman?"

DeKok did not answer. All his concentration was on guiding the car into the Warmoes Street. He stopped in front of the station.

"Let's reason together," he said seriously.

They walked past the desk sergeant and climbed the stairs to the detective room. The file on Brets was still spread out on DeKok's desk.

Vledder pulled up a chair.

"All right," he said, "first tell me who is Renard Kamperman and what has the good man done to attract your attention so suddenly?"

DeKok rubbed his face.

"He died," he answered simply.

"Died?"

"Yes, Renard Kamperman is the name of the man who was murdered tonight. Don't ask me how I know, because it would take too long to explain."

Vledder bit his lower lip.

"Do you know who did it?"

"What do you mean?"

"Who killed Kamperman?"

DeKok grinned without mirth.

"The same person who killed Jan Brets."

"What!?"

DeKok nodded.

"Yes, the same killer."

"And who might that be?"

Moodily, DeKok shrugged his shoulders.

"I don't know. I mean, I don't know *yet*! But I have some suspicions and I thought we have enough hints to discover his identity."

Vledder nodded pensively.

"Do you know *where* Kamperman was killed?"

DeKok shook his head, despair on his face.

"You're asking the same question my wife asked me an hour ago. It's a dumb question. Of course, I don't know where he's been murdered. If I had known that, I wouldn't have had to separate you from your Celine. You see, Dick, I think that Kamperman was killed because I discovered the motive for the murder of Jan Brets and also because Pierre Brassel needed a new alibi." He sounded irritated with himself. "I know it sounds like the raving of a lunatic, but that's the way it is."

Vledder sighed.

"Well, as I understand it, that means that Kamperman could have been killed anywhere. How do propose to figure that out?"

DeKok scratched the back of his neck.

"There's only one thing to do. We have to look, look for Kamperman. We'll find his corpse automatically, then. I see no other way. I checked. The last known address is eight years old."

Vledder grimaced.

"Eight years! He must have moved by now."

DeKok picked up the scattered pieces of the Brets file and threw them in a drawer.

"There's no choice," he said, a determined look on his face. "We have to check that address. It's our only starting point."

19

"What can I do for you?"

The young woman, her hand on the doorknob, looked shyly at the two men on the doorstep.

DeKok turned his hat in his hands, visibly embarrassed.

"Renard Kamperman?"

She looked at him suspiciously.

"That's my husband, yes."

DeKok rubbed the back of his hand along his dry lips and sighed.

"We would like to talk with you for a moment. My name is DeKok, with ... eh, kay-oh-kay. This is my colleague, Vledder. We're police inspectors ... Amsterdam police."

The woman brought her hands to her throat in an automatic reflex.

"Has something happened?" she asked fearfully.

DeKok lowered his head somewhat.

"No," he answered, hesitating. "That's to say ... we're not sure. Not exactly, I mean. It's all a bit difficult." He looked past her into the corridor. "Perhaps, we ... eh, we could better ... inside? It's a bit windy out."

She nodded, slightly dazed.

"Come in."

She opened the door wider. Everything looked clean, fresh and proper. Modern without frills. A tricycle in the corridor indicated a toddler and a rack with drying diapers told of a baby.

"We did have a little trouble finding you," said DeKok pleasantly. "Happily, one of your former neighbors remembered that your husband had taken a job with a large firm in Gouda. That's all she knew, but it was enough for us."

She offered the policemen a seat on a sofa.

"I don't know where my husband used to live." She sounded irked. "I don't want to know, either. We've been married four years and he's a good father." She looked at DeKok as if he was an enemy. "That's important, you see. To me, that's important."

Apparently she wanted to blot out her husband's past. A past she completely denied, but of which she was very well informed. DeKok was certain of that.

"Where is your husband?"

She did not answer.

"Where's your husband," repeated DeKok, more insistent.

She looked at him as if trying to read his thoughts.

"Don't you know?" she asked dubiously, suspicion in her voice.

DeKok shook his head.

"No, Mrs. Kamperman," he said affably, "we don't know where he is. Positively not. Believe me, we're not here to cause any problems. We're here as friends. As far as we know, your husband has not done anything illegal." He paused and sighed deeply. "Mrs. Kamperman," the tone of voice had changed, had a sad undertone, "I fear that your husband has been enticed to a specific place."

She blinked her eyes while she stared at him. Slowly she sank into an easy chair. She remained seated with her hands in her lap.

"Enticed?" she asked hoarsely.

DeKok nodded slowly.

"Yes," he said softly. "Enticed. I don't know how else to say it. I don't know how it happened, either. Perhaps he received a letter, or somebody approached him." He leaned toward her, to better see every possible reaction on her face. Then he asked: "Does the name Brassel mean anything to you?"

He saw the shock and a wave of pity overcame him. She knew about Brassel. No doubt she had heard the name and DeKok knew what that meant.

"Has Brassel been here, or did he write?"

She looked at him wildly.

"What's happened?" she cried, anxiety in her voice. "What do you want . . . what do you want with my husband? You said so yourself, he hasn't done a thing."

DeKok bit his lower lip.

"Mrs. Kamperman," he said soothingly, "Please tell me, where was your husband supposed to be, tonight at eight o'clock?"

She did not answer, but defiantly she pressed her lips together. DeKok sighed, but his expression remained friendly, indulgent, full of understanding.

"My dear Mrs. Kamperman," he said earnestly, "please believe me. In your own best interest, tell me where I can find your husband."

She shook her head.

"No." Her voice was determined and stubborn. "I won't tell. I promised not to talk about it."

DeKok swallowed.

"Mrs. Kamperman," he said. There was a dramatic, almost theatrical quality to his voice. "Upstairs," he stretched his hand toward the ceiling, "upstairs are two children, *your* children. They're asleep. I do hope sincerely that the poor dears may keep their father, but I'm afraid it's already too late."

It was as if a sudden understanding came over her, as if the deeper meaning of DeKok's words suddenly reached her. Her eyes widened, he breasts rose and fell rapidly. She panted.

"What's going on?" she wailed. "What's happened to my Renard?"

DeKok rubbed his tired eyes with a weary hand.

"I don't know," he admitted, bone tired. "Really, I don't know. But I do have a suspicion that something serious may have happened."

He stood up and placed a comforting hand on the young woman's shoulder.

"Please try to cooperate with us. Tell us honestly where your husband went tonight. Perhaps we won't be too late."

She lowered her head.

"He went to Amsterdam."

"Where?"

"The Greenland Arms, a hotel."

"The Greenland Arms?"

"Yes, he was to meet somebody there."

* * *

Renard Kamperman looked grotesque.

He was supine with arms and legs stretched out wide. It was as if he had wanted to cover as much of the floor space as possible. That's how they found him, in a strange position with pulled up knees and bent elbows. In that position he most resembled a wooden harlequin, a marionette of which all strings had been pulled up tight. A life-size harlequin. It would not have surprised DeKok in the least if the arms and legs had suddenly started to move rhythmically, as if guided by an unseen puppeteer pulling the strings. The image of a harlequin was so all pervasive. The waxen, almost white face of Renard Kamperman was frozen into a grinning, partly surprised grimace, as if he did not understand something, as if his own, sudden death was a huge joke of which he had just missed the punch line.

The complete picture was silly, ridiculous, but not macabre, or fearsome. Death presented itself mildly, without horror. A cursory examination did not even show any overt signs of violence. Just a small trickle of blood from the left ear, ending in an already coagulated puddle on the floor. That was all.

"Dammit," exclaimed the concierge of the Greenland Arms, shocked. "Well, dammit, only ... only the guy is different."

DeKok nodded.

"The guy is different," he repeated pensively, "yes, only the victim has changed."

He looked at Vledder who was busy taking notes and measurements. It was if time had stood still, as if the world had not turned, as if the sun had not set and then risen again. It was an uncanny feeling.

With a long face, hands in his pockets, he looked around, searching for differences. There were no differences. Everything was exactly the same. Except for the victim.

He walked out of the room and counted the number of paces to the elevator. There were thirty paces, back and forth. When he was again in front of the door, he realized there should have been at least one more difference. He looked up. The number 21 was painted on the door.

Wildly he took the concierge by an arm.

"Why," he cried, furious. "Why was this room rented? Who had the unmitigated gall to break the seals?"

The concierge looked at him, astonishment on his face.

"But we were told we could."

"By whom?"

The concierge swallowed.

"Your ... eh, your own chief, the Commissaris."

"What!?"

"Yes, your own Commissaris. Our director called several times to ask if the seals could be removed."

DeKok stared at him.

"Your director called personally?' His eyes narrowed.

The concierge nodded vehemently.

"Yes, yes. I was there myself. Several times. Always to the Commissaris in the Warmoes Street. The first time was shortly after you had placed the seals. His request was denied. He cursed a blue streak."

"And?"

"During the following days he called regularly. Apparently he finally got permission yesterday afternoon. To break the seals, I mean. Anyway, he issued immediate instructions to remove the seals and to ready the room for occupancy." He made a helpless gesture. "So, of course, I did as I was told."

DeKok nodded.

"Yes, of course, I understand." He rubbed the bridge of his nose with his little finger. "I don't think," he began thoughtfully, "that I met your director, the last time, did I?"

The concierge shook his head.

"No, the director didn't come down until after you and your colleague had left. He lives upstairs, you see. In the penthouse suite. Since his illness he doesn't concern himself with the actual running of the business as much. It's usually left in the hands of the department heads and the Assistant Manager. But somebody probably told him what happened."

"Who?"

"Not me."

"Who, then?"

The concierge shrugged his shoulders.

"I don't know, could have been anybody, even a bellhop, or a chambermaid."

DeKok sighed.

"How did he react. I mean, wasn't he upset that the name of his hotel was getting such notoriety?"

Slowly the concierge shook his head.

"He didn't say anything about it. He just asked me what had happened after he had found out. I told him as much as I knew, also about the sealing of the room."

DeKok nodded slowly to himself.

"The list you gave me last time, I mean the list of personnel. Wasn't the name of the director on that list?"

The concierge grinned.

"No," he said indignantly, "he's the director, of course he wasn't on it."

DeKok hid his face in his hands and groaned.

20

Inspector DeKok looked searchingly around. Room 21 of the Greenland Arms looked normal again. The nervous activity of the police had ceased and the corpse of Renard Kamperman had been removed. Only a small bloodstain was still visible, the only remaining evidence of the crime.

"Are you finished?"

Vledder looked at the room one more time and nodded.

"I thinks so," he said, hesitating. "I don't think I missed anything." He took his notebook and read through his notes. "No," he concluded, "I've done everything I can, I think."

DeKok nodded approvingly.

"Excellent, really excellent. Then you better go."

Vledder pointed at the door.

"What about the seals?"

DeKok shrugged his shoulders with a tired gesture.

"Ach, no." His voice was lethargic. "Leave it. It makes no difference, not anymore. We know everything. Anyway, there won't be any more murders, not here. This was the last vengeance of the harlequin."

Vledder looked at him in confusion.

"You seem convinced about that."

DeKok nodded with a haggard face.

"Yes, I am," he sighed. "Convinced and very sad." He gave Vledder a wan smile. "Come on, Dick, it'll be so late, otherwise." He looked at his watch. "You can be in Gouda in no time. Be careful, don't speed. And be careful, there. I mean, try to tell Mrs. Kamperman as gently as possible. She's going to be upset enough, as it is. She needs to be told very gently. She doesn't need any extra shocks. Tell her the kids no longer have a father. Tell her she's a widow, but be very gentle. Try to comfort her as best you can. Locate relatives. But she needs to be told."

Vledder smiled uncomfortably.

"Without shocking her," he repeated bitterly. "I'd much rather you came with me. You're so much better in those situations. I never know how to handle someone else's sorrow. I usually get all upset myself."

DeKok slapped him lightly on the shoulder in a fatherly, comforting way.

"That doesn't matter, Dick," he said. "Nothing against that. Sorrow is universal."

Vledder sighed.

"You're really not coming along?"

DeKok shook his head.

"I'm staying here."

"In the hotel?"

"For the time being. I promised myself an interview with the director."

Vledder nodded.

"Well, alright, then," he said with a melancholy face, "I'm off, then. Tell you the truth, I don't look forward to it. I can just picture what'll be waiting for me in Gouda. A crying woman and screaming kids. I hope she has family nearby. Otherwise I may have to wake the neighbors."

DeKok nodded.

"Do the best you can," he said simply.

* * *

A gruff expression on his face, his old felt hat far back on the back of his head, DeKok stood in front of the concierge's desk and rapped on the wood with a flat hand. An immovable object, a stubborn force of nature.

Startled, the concierge looked up.

"Oh," he stammered, confused, "I didn't know you were still on the premises. I thought you'd left at the same time as your colleague."

DeKok grinned maliciously.

"No, my friend," he said threateningly, "I'm still here. I stayed behind, stayed to have a nice little chat with your director."

"Oh," said the concierge.

"Yes," answered DeKok. "Now will you be so kind as to announce me?"

The concierge sighed deeply.

"Mr. Gosler," he hesitated, "is ill. Very ill, I might say. For months now, he hasn't received anyone in his suite. And most certainly not at this hour. It's well past midnight."

DeKok forced his lips into a broad smile.

"I know what time it is, my friend," he remarked with syrupy sarcasm, "you don't have to tell me." He shook his gray head. "Anyway, I didn't ask you the time at all, at all. I just asked you to announce me to your director. That's all."

The concierge pulled his head between his shoulders.

"I'm afraid," he said, avoiding the issue, "that . . ."

That is as far as he progressed.

DeKok leaned over the desk and in a casual, but irresistible way, he grabbed the man by the neck and pulled him from behind his desk.

"Come, friend," he hissed, "show me the way."

The concierge struggled in DeKok's grip.

"If you'll permit me," he squeaked, "I'll call ahead. That would be better, I think."

DeKok released him.

"Excellent, really excellent, my friend. Call him first. But be sure to let him know that I *insist* on speaking with him."

DeKok raised a cautioning finger.

"And, just in case, if mister-the-director has some exalted, but mistaken, idea of his own importance that may lead him to believe that he can keep me out, or cooling my heels, you tell him for me that he is grossly in error. If necessary, I will personally and extremely unlawfully, but nevertheless inevitably, break down his door."

The concierge studied DeKok's determined face and swallowed nervously.

"Really," he exclaimed, impressed and scared, "I really believe you'd do that."

DeKok grimaced.

"You can bet your life."

* * *

"I shall seriously complain about you. You may depend on that. The Commissaris in the Warmoes Street is a personal friend of mine. It is simply unheard of that you should bother a seriously ill person in the middle of the night. It's simply not done. You haven't the right. You're acting outside the law. You're overreaching yourself. You overstep your authority, yes, you're far exceeding your authority."

DeKok nodded toward the man seated across from him in an easy chair and gave him a pitying smile. The stern look with which the director had meant to reinforce his message came from a set of tired, weary eyes. His behavior was no more than a sad demonstration of physical debilitation. He rested his head against the high back of the chair and sighed.

DeKok looked at him, outwardly unmoved. The sharp gaze searched the face intently, looking for a family resemblance. It was there, undeniably so. The blond hair. The blue eyes. A pair of long, skinny hands, deformed by arthritis, emerged from the sleeves of the robe which seemed several sizes too big. DeKok judged him to be about fifty years of age, but realized immediately that the opinion was based on a hunch, not the physical evidence. The face was wan, marked by a stealthy disease that had left indelible signs of its progress. Fredrich Gosler seemed at least fifteen years older than his true age.

"It's strange," sighed DeKok, "really strange. Everybody connected to this case knows exactly how to tell me the limits of my authority. In addition, a lot has been said about 'justice', almost from the start." He shook his head, displeased. "You see, especially the last bothers me no end. History should have taught us: Just before a war, peace is the main topic of conversation."

Mr. Gosler leaned forward.

"I don't understand you," he said softly.

DeKok grinned his irresistible grin.

"I do believe that your intelligent brother-in-law *would* have understood me, Mr. Gosler. What I mean to say is that most wars are waged in the name of peace and a lot of *injustice* seems to be practiced in the name of *justice*."

For a long time Mr. Gosler looked at him thoughtfully.

"You . . . ," he faltered, ". . you know the motive?"

DeKok did not answer at once. He rubbed the corners of his eyes with thumb and index finger. It was a tired gesture. A sudden lethargy overcame him. It was if the tension under which he had worked for the last few days had suddenly snapped, as if the adrenaline flow had been cut off. He felt he had reached his goal, but could not enjoy the moment, on the contrary, it made him feel extremely depressed.

"Yes," he answered after a long pause. "I know your motive."

"And?"

"What?"

"Well, what do you think of the motive?"

DeKok swallowed.

"I'm sorry," he said, shaking his head, "but no matter how you slice it, I cannot admire it."

Gosler's face fell. His fingers cramped around the armrests of the chair. The knuckles showed up white. Slowly he pushed himself into a standing position.

With his arms tightly pressed against his body, tense, almost as if he was on parade, he stood in front of DeKok.

"Then, inspector," he spoke formally, "you must arrest me at once."

DeKok looked up, gazed at the scarecrow figure in the wide robe that hung around the man in large folds, the dull, sunken eyes, the shallow cheeks, and shook his head.

"No," he answered slowly, "I don't think I will."

Gosler looked at him in surprise.

"But you *must* arrest me," he cried out. "I insist, it's your duty."

DeKok shrugged his shoulders in a careless gesture.

"Ach, Mr. Gosler," he said moodily, "please sit down. You're much too ill to stand for long. In addition, you cannot order me. And as far as my duty is concerned, *I* will determine what that is."

The hotel director hesitated an instant longer. Then he lowered himself shakily back into his chair. His face was gray and DeKok realized how much effort it must have taken the man to handle the heavy hockey stick with such deadly effect. Gosler seemed to read his mind.

"I'm losing ground rapidly, especially these last few days." It sounded hopeless. "But I'm glad I was able to complete my task. I was afraid that I would not be able to do so."

He paused and sighed.

"But I do insist that you place me into custody. The world may know what I have done and why."

DeKok looked at him sharply.

"No, Mr. Gosler," he said, shaking his head. "The world may *not* know. The world must never know. If your motives were to become common knowledge, there will be too many people, shortsighted people, like you, who will find your motives acceptable. And perhaps there will be a few, among these shortsighted people, who are in the same circumstances as you. I mean, who cannot be touched by human justice, because of illness."

An ugly grin appeared on the small mouth of Gosler.

"If you don't arrest me, I'll call the Commissaris. If he doesn't respond, there's always the press."

DeKok nodded morosely.

"I take it," he said, "that my Commissaris is not yet informed?"

"Not yet."

DeKok stared a long time at nothing at all. There was a resigned, almost sphinx-like, look on his face. After a few minutes he stood up. He took the ivory colored phone from a side table and placed it in the lap of the astonished Gosler. Then he sat down again and gave the sick man a friendly, challenging nod.

"You know the number of my chief?"

Confused, Gosler nodded.

"Excellent," said DeKok, "really excellent. Then you may call him now."

Gosler looked at him suspiciously.

"Now . . .?"

DeKok gestured.

"But of course. Why not? But I should point out to you that the moment you talk to the Commissaris, or inform the press, I will go directly to Oldwater. There I will take your sister and your brother-in-law in custody. Please note, *regardless* of the children."

He paused.

"And please, Mr. Gosler," he continued, "do not think for one single moment that they will get off scot-free. Laws, rules and norms will only guarantee a free society as long as everybody lives accordingly, you see, Mr. Gosler. If necessary, I will perjure myself. If once is not enough, I will perjure myself again and again. Please disabuse yourself of any ideas about my trustworthiness, my honesty. If I have to, I can be just like you, a man without any scruples."

Gosler's eyes narrowed.

"Is that a threat?"

"You can take it any way you want. Just be certain of this: if you confess as the perpetrator, or make public your deeds in any way, your sister and your brother-in-law will go to jail as accessories before, during and *after* the fact."

Gosler studied his face for a long time, gauging the seriousness of the threat.

"Yes," he concluded finally, "you would."

Grinning, DeKok picked up the telephone from Gosler's lap and replaced it out of reach.

"Come," he said in a friendly tone of voice, "let us speak about justice."

Gosler gave him a tired nod.

21

Furious, the Commissaris clawed for the phone. The report about the murder was in front of him. It was an extremely short report, no more than half a page. It contained the information that the corpse of a man had been found in Room 21 of the Greenland Arms. The man was identified as Renard Kamperman, age 26, and the circumstances surrounding the body showed a marked similarity to those found at the time when the corpse of Jan Johannes Brets was discovered. That was the sum-total of the content. That was all. The Commissaris was extremely displeased with it. He banged his fist on the desk and yelled loudly into the telephone:

"Have DeKok report to me!"

Inspector Corstant, who happened to pick up the telephone in the detective room, remarked calmly that he could not understand the speaker.

"Have DeKok report to me," repeated the Commissaris, calmer.

"I'm sorry," replied Corstant.

"What?"

"DeKok isn't here."

"What about Vledder?"

"He's here."

"Good, have Vledder report."

"As you wish," replied Corstant quietly. He replaced the receiver and looked around. When he spotted Vledder he motioned him closer.

"The boss wants you, Dick. Better take a deep breath, he's really pissed."

Vledder shrugged his shoulders.

"It's not my fault." Vledder smirked. "I've always been real nice to him." He put his jacket on, arranged his tie and left to meet his boss.

The Commissaris was beside himself. He paced up and down his office like a caged lion and vented his torrent of anger and frustration on poor Vledder.

"Two murders in three days," he roared, "and what does it get me?" He banged the desk with his fist every time he passed by it. "What do I have to show for it? Eh? Answer me that! I'll tell you what I have. Two minuscule reports, *that's* what I have! And what's in those reports, eh? I'll tell you what's in those reports. Nothing! Jackshit!" He raised both arms despairingly toward the ceiling. "What *have* you two accomplished, for crying out loud! Am I perhaps privileged to know? Eh? So, tell me already, who's the boss around here? Eh? DeKok or me!?"

Vledder dared a cautious remark.

"You are, Commissaris."

"Right," hollered the Commissaris, "I am! *I* know that and *you* know that! But does DeKok know that? Eh? Why don't you ask him!?"

Vledder swallowed.

"I will, sir," answered Vledder earnestly.

The Commissaris controlled himself and sat down behind his desk. Venting his rage had soothed his nerves. He was visibly relieved, more relaxed. He stroked his gray hair with a steady hand and indicated to Vledder that he was allowed to sit down.

"Three murders in two days," he lamented.

"Two murders in three days," corrected Vledder.

The Commissaris gestured impatiently.

"Yes, well, that's what I mean. And both murders in the same hotel. In the same room, even. There has to be a connection, you know. It's too much of a coincidence. You were there, weren't you, I mean with Brets *and* Kamperman?"

Vledder nodded.

"Both times," he admitted.

"And ... eh, what does DeKok say about it?"

"DeKok is never too forthcoming in that sort of situation. But I did get the impression that he was close to a solution. That's to say, he mentioned that he had sufficient evidence to discover the killer."

The Commissaris nodded thoughtfully.

"So, is that what he said?"

"Yes, sir. And DeKok isn't a braggart. If DeKok says that ..."

The Commissaris did not want to hear anymore praise. He stood up and from beneath his bushy eyebrows he looked down on Vledder with a penetrating look.

"Have DeKok report to me."

It was an order.

Vledder made an apologetic movement with his hands.

"I really don't know where he is. I called his home this morning, but he isn't there. I spoke to his wife. She doesn't know where he is, either."

The commissarial face was getting dangerously red. He stretched his arm in the direction of the door.

"Then you find him, for all I care you put out an APB on him, but find him!"

It echoed through the room.

Vledder nodded.

"Yessir," he said timidly, "yessir, I will."

Then he fled from the room.

* * *

DeKok guided his own, personal VW through the old inner city of Amsterdam. He had just come from an extended visit with Dr. Brouchec and now he was hunting for a parking spot as close as possible to the respectable firm of Brassel & Son, Certified Public Accountants.

The interview with the doctor had confirmed his opinion about Fredrich Gosler's illness. Gosler, too, had no illusions.

At first the good doctor had been reluctant to cooperate. But when DeKok threatened with the arrest of Fredrich Gosler and then described the conditions in the cells at the Warmoes Street in lurid detail, the doctor had relented. In the strictest confidence, so he told DeKok, he had shared his medical opinion and prognosis. DeKok had asked for a written statement, but the doctor had categorically refused that.

"Just wait," he had said.

But it was exactly the waiting that put DeKok in a difficult predicament.

When he finally found a place for his car, he got out and ambled over to the Brassel office. His face was serious. The creases in his forehead were deeper and sharper than usual. He had a plan, but he knew the risks involved. He also knew that his official instructions, a booklet with several supplements, mentioned specific official responses to the situation. But DeKok had no special love for rules and regulations. He liked people. The conflicts between the needs of people and the official guidelines were not always easily reconciled.

He climbed the bluestone steps to the front door and rang the old-fashioned, brass bell-pull. After about a minute the heavy, black lacquered door was opened. A green-eyed girl confronted him. There was a dimple in her left cheek. DeKok lifted his hat with a flourish and smiled.

"My name is DeKok," he said amiably, "DeKok with ... eh, kay-oh-kay. Please tell Mr. Brassel I want to speak to him."

* * *

A bit shyly, Vledder adjusted his tie.

"Mrs. DeKok," he said, beseechingly, "do you really not know where your husband is? The Commissaris is furious, he's yelling and screaming that he wants DeKok. Justifiably so, I think. I mean, Mrs. DeKok, you know how I like your husband, but he hasn't been in the office for more than three days. That's absurd, let's face it."

Mrs. DeKok nodded.

"You're right, Dick, it *is* absurd. I can't understand myself, what's come over him." She laughed at him. "Of course I know where he is. But he told me that he wasn't available to anyone."

Vledder pulled a hurt face.

"Not even to me?"

She smiled tenderly.

"Come back at eight tonight, Dick. I'll make sure he's here."

* * *

DeKok greeted his young colleague heartily. He shook his hand for a long time, placed a friendly arm around his shoulder and led him to the cozy living room. DeKok's face beamed. He seemed genuinely please about Vledder's visit.

"I do believe, Dick," he said jovially, "that I owe you an explanation. Of course, I would have told you everything when the time came, but my wife took pity on you and persuaded me to explain everything now."

Mrs. DeKok winked at Vledder.

"Really," she said with a smile, "it wasn't all that hard."

"But my wife is right," added DeKok seriously, "why not, after all? We've been working together for some time. I know I can trust you." He gestured. "And I need that trust, you see, I must ask you to keep things secret. You can't talk about anything of what I'm about to tell you to anybody, for the time being. Not even the Commissaris, especially not the Commissaris. You must understand that I'm not avoiding him for nothing."

Vledder looked surprised.

"Is he involved?"

DeKok laughed.

"No, not really, thank goodness. But if he knew the whole story, he might force me to arrest the murderer. And I don't want to."

Vledder looked at him with disbelief.

"You don't want to?"

DeKok shook his head.

"No, I don't want to. I've a number of reasons for that, reasons I'll try to explain in the course of the evening."

He pointed at some comfortable, leather armchairs.

"Come on, Dick, pull up a pew."

212

He walked over to the side board and returned with a bottle of French Cognac. He showed the label.

"What do you think?"

Vledder nodded wholehearted approval of the choice.

DeKok took a couple of large snifters and warmed them gently over a small flame. Then he poured with total concentration. DeKok loved good cognac, he was a connoisseur. He enjoyed it with gusto. The stimulating aroma, the tantalizing taste, the warming glow. A good glass of cognac was almost a sensuous pleasure to DeKok, total bliss, pure delight.

"I have," he started after his first sip, "made a lot of mistakes in this case. Mistakes are almost inevitable in our profession. During every investigation, especially at the start, one gropes. Every step, no matter how carefully taken, can lead in the wrong direction. But a person should not be afraid to make mistakes. I mean, when you're afraid to make mistakes, you'll avoid all decisions, circumvent facts and eventually you'll be reduced to fearful inaction altogether. No, Dick, I've never been afraid to make mistakes, I've never dodged decisions."

He took another sip and replaced his glass carefully.

"But, to business," he continued. "From the first it was certain that Pierre Brassel couldn't possibly be the perpetrator. His alibi, for both murders, was incontrovertible, untouchable. Of course, everything pointed to the fact that he had to be in contact with the killer, that he was completely aware of his plans and that he sympathized with those plans, cooperated with those plans. But who was the real murderer? Who was the man *behind* Brassel? Intriguing questions, to say the least. But what occupied me most of all, was the *why*! Why was Jan Brets killed? Why did Brassel play his dangerous game that bordered on outright complicity? In other words: What was the motive?"

He glanced at Vledder, moved himself more comfortably in his chair. His hand strayed to the glass beside him, but he controlled the movement. He went on:

"Most of the usual motives didn't seem to apply. They just didn't fit. They didn't compute, as you said. There was no connection between Brets and Brassel, at least not a connection that would imply a motive. The murder seemed just senseless. But Brets was not an accidental victim, on the contrary. Brets was carefully selected as the victim. He was sought out by Brassel and enticed to take a room at the Greenland Arms."

DeKok raised an index finger in the air.

"What had decided that choice? I mean, why Brets? After all, he wasn't much more than a relatively unimportant burglar from Utrecht, right? Who would benefit from his death? As I said, there was no direct connection between Brets and Brassel. Therefore there had to be an *indirect* connection, an *indirect* motive. How? The only possibility was through the man behind Brassel, via the *real* killer. But who was that?" DeKok grinned. "I kept thinking like that, in circles, always the same questions."

"I haven't heard any mistakes, yet," observed Vledder.

DeKok sighed.

"That'll come. As you will remember, the day after the murder of Brets, we visited Brassel in Oldwater and met his wife. Because of certain remarks, but more so because of her behavior, her attitude, I received the distinct impression that the real murderer could be found within the family circle of the Brassels. It was a good hunch, it would certainly provide a reasonable explanation for Pierre's behavior. After all, for your family you make sacrifices. So why

214

wouldn't Pierre play his little games to help a family member?"

DeKok made a grand gesture.

"*If* I had continued that train of thought, at the time, I *might* have been able to prevent the murder of Renard Kamperman."

Vledder, his drink forgotten, looked at his mentor with astonishment.

"But why didn't you?"

DeKok gave Vledder a weary smile.

"Simply because I overestimated the intelligence of Brassel, and his knowledge of the law."

"I don't follow you."

DeKok grinned ruefully.

"Do you remember we discussed the so-called warning note that night? Brassel became visibly upset when I lied to him and told him we hadn't found it under the corpse of Brets? From his reaction I concluded that Brassel placed an inordinate amount of importance on this warning note. And he did!"

DeKok sighed deeply.

"At that time I came to the wrong conclusion. You see, if the real killer was within the family circle, Brassel didn't have to warn anybody. But he *did* warn Brets and therefore I concluded that the real perpetrator was *not* a member of his family."

Mrs. DeKok leaned toward her husband.

"You mean," she said slowly, "that Brassel wouldn't have had to write a warning note if the killer was a member of his own family?"

DeKok nodded.

"That's right. He didn't have to inform the police, nor the intended victim, because, since it concerned his own family, he could have invoked the Right of Extenuation."

"Right of Extenuation?"

"Yes, that's what we call it here. According to Dutch Law, nobody has to cooperate in the criminal prosecution of a blood relative. Most countries have something similar. The best known example is the American Fifth Amendment. It states that nobody is required to testify against himself, or herself. Well, the laws in most countries also specify that a husband doesn't have to testify against his wife, or vice versa. Things like that. The Dutch Law goes them one better. In Holland, the so-called Fifth Amendment Rights, extend to self and all relatives in the first degree, wives, sons, daughters, parents, brothers, sisters, whatever. Anyway, Brassel either did not know that, or did not understand that. It doesn't matter, I was misled, regardless."

Vledder looked at him searchingly.

"Misled?" he asked.

DeKok rubbed his face with both hands.

"Yes," he sighed, "the murderer *was* a member of his immediate family."

Mrs. DeKok rose from her chair.

"How about some coffee?" she proposed.

DeKok nodded agreement with a regretful glance at the bottle of cognac. He lifted his glass and drained it. Then he poured himself another measure and raised his eyebrows at Vledder. Vledder hastily agreed that a refill would be most welcome.

Mrs. DeKok watched with an indulgent smile.

"Well, what about coffee?" she repeated.

"Yes, darling," said DeKok, "and some of that cake, you know, from Mrs. Brassel's recipe."

Mrs. DeKok looked at him with mocking eyes.

"Why don't you call it *harlequin cake*?"

DeKok laughed briefly.

"Yes," he smiled at his wife, "why not? Coffee and Harlequin."

Vledder could hardly contain his impatience. The intermezzo was something he could have done without. He would much rather listen to DeKok unravel the rest of the story, but he knew full well that the gray sleuth was not to be hurried.

Mrs. DeKok returned in due course with coffee and cake. Meanwhile she chatted cheerfully about the fantastic recipe from Mrs. Brassel. The atmosphere was relaxed as if murders and their solutions were the farthest thing from their minds. Finally Vledder could stand it no longer. He edged closer to the front of his chair.

"How," he asked with barely contained impatience, "did you discover that the killer was a member of the family?"

"Hampelmann."

Vledder did not understand the cryptic remark.

"Hampelmann?"

DeKok nodded.

"Yes, the German word for Harlequin."

"It doesn't mean a thing to me," replied Vledder, annoyed. "The only thing I know is that both Brets and Kamperman were found in a position that reminded one of a harlequin. What's that got to do with German?"

DeKok sighed.

"But that's the point. Harlequin, in German: Hampelmann. The corpses were purposely arranged in that position."

"But why?"

DeKok smiled faintly.

"As a symbol."

"Symbol? Symbol of what?"

"Justice."

"Justice?"

"Yes, Dick, justice. But to understand it, we have to go back in time a little"

He drained his cup and Mrs. DeKok almost immediately refilled it. He started:

"A few years before World War II, a certain Heinrich Gosler was arrested by the Nazis. Gosler's wife, a Jewish girl, managed to flee to Holland with her two small children. She went to Haarlem, where her brother, Jacob Hampelmann, who had fled years earlier, had settled and started an antique business. Apparently in the hope of doing something for her husband and at considerable risk to herself, Frau Gosler returned to Germany after about a month. She was probably picked up shortly after that and nothing further was ever heard of the Goslers, husband, or wife. As far as is known, they perished in a concentration camp."

He paused briefly, reflected.

"The two children, Fredrich and Liselotte," he resumed, "stayed in Haarlem with Uncle Hampelmann who took care of them as if they were his own, and who provided them with an excellent education. How he managed to do that under the circumstances, under the noses of the German occupation forces, would make a heroic saga, no doubt. But he managed, one way or the other. Naturally the children were devoted to Uncle Hampelmann."

Thoughtfully he rubbed the bridge of his nose with his little finger. Vledder and Mrs. DeKok hung on his every word.

"But, about eight years ago Jan Brets and Renard Kamperman met in one of our incomparable reform institutions. Both boys, seventeen and eighteen at the time, had been placed there by a juvenile court. Jan Brets because he had endangered life and property around Utrecht and Kamperman as the result of a series of burglaries in and around Haarlem, including a failed attempt on the establishment of Hampelmann. Brets and Kamperman exchanged experiences and ideas and Kamperman told about Hampelmann who, so it was generally believed, was a rich man. The trouble was, according to Kamperman, that the old antique dealer was 'as alert as a bloody watchdog'. But Brets had a remedy for that."

He sighed deeply. Then he continued:

"Oh, yes, Brets knew how to fix that. If he got his hands on the old man, he'd never again be alert. In fact, he'd never wake up again. So, while still in reform school, these two planned a cold-blooded robbery with murder. The very next week-end, for which they had received a pass as the result of 'good behavior', they hitch-hiked to Haarlem, bought a hammer on the way, and bashed in old Hampelmann's head that same night. The total proceeds of the robbery amounted to less than ten dollars."

Mrs. DeKok shook her head in horrified astonishment.

"But that's terrible," she exclaimed.

"Indeed, terrible. Fredrich and Liselotte were extremely upset, to say the least. They were devastated. Neither was at home when it happened. Fredrich worked in a hotel, where he was being groomed for management and Liselotte was staying with Pierre Brassel, still her fiancee at the time. Anyway, Brets and Kamperman were soon found and they confessed. During the investigation it was discovered that the old man must have defended himself strenuously against his attackers. Brets had hit him so many times with the hammer that the end was inevitable. When Fredrich Gosler heard the details, he went into a savage rage and he swore that he would avenge his uncle's murder."

"The seed for later murders." interrupted Vledder.

"Exactly," agreed DeKok, "the seed had been planted for more murders."

They remained silent. It was as if Fredrich Gosler's vengeful hate had taken possession of them, as if the murders were being contemplated anew.

Mrs. DeKok moved uneasily in her chair.

"You know," she said earnestly, "I can understand how Fredrich Gosler would come to think that way. If, at the time, he could have laid hands on those two guys, an emotional murder could have been understood, not justified, mind you, but understood. But now . . . eight years later . . ."

DeKok bit his lower lip thoughtfully.

"You're right. Then . . . yes, maybe. But Brets and Kamperman went to jail and Gosler's rage cooled off. But he did keep an eye on those two and then he learned that not much was left of the original punishment. Our much touted system of parole and rehabilitation, you know. A few years later the killers of Uncle Hampelmann were as free as a bird. As you'll understand, Fredrich Gosler wasn't happy at all, at all. He considered it a miscarriage of justice. He discussed it with his sister and his brother-in-law, Pierre Brassel. All three were agreed that no justice had been done to Uncle Hampelmann and Fredrich proposed the idea of murder as a belated execution."

Vledder looked up.

"That sounds familiar."

DeKok nodded.

"Yes, I guess it would. Pierre Brassel made a mistake, right at the beginning. That was during our first meeting at the station. He was wondering out loud why he should take risks for murder like that, . . . eh, . . . *which is no more than a somewhat belated . . .*" DeKok smiled. "You remember? He swallowed the last word, but the word was meant to be *execution.*"

Mrs. DeKok made a vague gesture.

"So, they accepted Gosler's idea at once?" she asked.

"No, Pierre Brassel was against it. He didn't want to go through with it. You understand, he was really an outsider, after all. He thought a lot more soberly about vengeance than brother and sister Gosler. He thought it was a stupid idea to risk their lives, their position, for murder of the likes of Brets and Kamperman, inferior beings in his eyes. Not worthy of the attentions of a gentleman. Beneath them, you know."

"B-but . . . ," stuttered Vledder, "*then* what happened? I don't understand. The killings took place after all."

"Yes, but for a different reason," said DeKok.

"A different reason?"

"Cancer."

He remained silent. In his mind's eye he saw again the sick man. The dull eyes, the hollow cheeks, the half paralyzed mouth that spoke of justice.

"Yes," he continued, "Fredrich Gosler became ill with cancer and a forthright doctor told him that he had maybe six months left."

DeKok rubbed his eyes with a thumb and an index finger.

"The rest is easily figured out. Gosler decide to use the last six month of his life to avenge the murder of his uncle,

221

to do him justice. He asked for the help of his brother-in-law, Pierre Brassel."

Mrs. DeKok gave him a compassionate look.

"And," she asked, "this time Brassel was willing to cooperate?"

"Brassel was in a difficult position. In principle he agreed with his wife's brother. Uncle Hampelmann had not received justice. But he was still not inclined to take unnecessary risks for futile vengeance. Also, by nature he was a lot more humane. Brassel believed that the criminals could be rehabilitated, maybe *had* been rehabilitated. He didn't think that Brets, after all those years, was still the same murderous maniac he had been when he bashed in the head of Uncle Hampelmann. He pleaded for a test."

"A test?" asked Vledder.

"Yes, a test. Jan Brets would be placed in a hypothetical situation, where he would have the same choice."

"The same choice?"

"Yes," answered DeKok patiently, "a situation where Brets would have to make a choice between killing ... and not killing."

"Ah, I get it. The old watchman."

"Exactly. Brassel approached Brets with a lot of garbage about a gang, an organization ..." He raised his index finger in the air. " ... and a rich haul at Bunsum & Company. He suggested that the old night watchman would have to be neutralized, eliminated, and he supplied Brets with the weapon to be used, the lead reinforced hockey stick. It was clear that anybody who was hit on the head with *that* instrument, would not survive the experience. But Brets cheerfully accepted the stick and the assignment. He declared to have no qualms about taking care of the old man."

"And thus he signed his own death warrant."

"Indeed, Brets had failed the test."

Mrs. DeKok was visibly upset. She shook her head, as if to clear it. A cold-blooded test to determine if someone was to be killed, or not. It was more than she could bear.

"But what about Kamperman?" she cried.

"Pierre Brassel had no further arguments to delay matters," he answered somberly. "Perhaps he could have delayed the vengeance by pointing out the risks to him personally, but the disease, the illness of Gosler had taken away all such arguments. It had taken enough arguing to get Gosler to agree to the test in the first place. And Jan Brets was as ready to commit murder now, as he had been in the past."

DeKok shook his head in despair.

"When Brassel asked for a test with Kamperman," he continued, "Gosler didn't want to hear about it. Time was pressing, you see. Fredrich Gosler was getting weaker by the day. The disease progressed faster than the doctor had estimated. If he was to complete his self-imposed task, they had to hurry."

"So, Renard Kamperman didn't have a chance?"

It sounded bitter.

"That's the most tragical part of the whole situation, because Kamperman *had* been rehabilitated. He had turned over a new leaf, moved from his old surroundings and married. He and his wife had two small children and he had become a respectable father, husband and wage earner."

DeKok stopped talking. His final words still hung in the room.

After a long silence, Mrs. DeKok spoke.

"Justice can be a terrible word," she said.

DeKok pushed his lower lip forward and nodded.

"Sometimes," he agreed bitterly.

Vledder was still deep in thought.

"Why," he asked after a while, "Don't you finish this case in the normal, prescribed manner?"

"What do you mean?"

"Well, arrest Gosler."

"No, I won't do that. Please understand, not because of Gosler, or because of his illness. Certainly not because I sympathize with his motives, but because I'm afraid."

"You? Afraid?"

"Yes, I'm afraid of the consequences. You see, cancer is not exactly a rare disease. Suppose that everybody, when they know the end is near, starts to take justice in their own hands. Starts a private execution business. The consequences don't bear thinking about. That's why it's better if the case of the dead harlequins will never be public knowledge."

* * *

It was already late at night when Vledder went home.

"Say hello to the office for me, tomorrow," said DeKok in parting.

Vledder smiled.

"When are you coming back?"

"As soon as Fredrich Gosler has passed on. According to the doctor it's only a matter of days. Not until then will I report to the Commissaris."

He made a simple gesture, shrugged his shoulders.

"You cannot arrest the dead."

Epilogue

There will be few important murders which are so characterized by a dearth of reports and documentation as happened to a case which is filed in the dusty attics of the Palace of Justice on the Prince's Canal in Amsterdam under case number PJ9786/117.

The entire file of the murder, a small gray folder, contains just two summary reports, two opinions by a forensic pathologist and a short note, written in a fluid, legible handwriting.

And that is all.

For anyone familiar with the world of Justice and the legal profession, which are by no means always the same, no matter what country or jurisdiction is involved, it will be almost incomprehensible that so few documents were considered sufficient to "close the case".

It is positively impossible to re-construct what really happened from the contents of the folder. The documentation is simply too scarce. One cannot escape the suspicion that the detective who handled the case at the time was less than frank and must have hidden, or destroyed, important documents. He must have deliberately remained silent on specific aspects of the case.

Therefore, the few hints which *are* present in the folder, gain a certain interest. They become more peculiar and serve to shroud the entire episode in a veil of mystique. What remains with the reader, after closing the file, is a strange empty feeling, an irritating desire to know more. It is as if a dinner is interrupted after the taste stimulating appetizers have been served, leaving one hungry for the main course that never materializes. Perhaps even that is an incomplete simile. Perhaps a "murder" is too serious a subject for that sort of comparison. But whatever the cause, the tantalizing feeling of emptiness remains. The desire to know. It becomes a challenge by its very incompleteness. For instance, the note. A ridiculous letter. Almost! But just the short, laconic content stimulates curiosity. It is extremely disturbing that the remaining documents in the folder are unable to satisfy that curiosity. There are missing links, gaps in the complete picture. One cannot help but wonder about the what and the wherefore. Murders are not committed at a whim, at least not usually. Somewhere underlying the thoughts of the murderer must be a motive. But what motive? As stated, the folder gives no explanations.

About the Author:

Albert Cornelis Baantjer (BAANTJER) is the most widely read author in the Netherlands. In a country with less than 15 million inhabitants, almost one out of every four people has bought a Baantjer book. More than 40 titles in his "DeKok" series have been written and almost 4 million copies have been sold. Baantjer can safely be considered a publishing phenomenon. In addition he has written other fiction and non-fiction and writes a daily column for a Dutch newspaper. It is for his "DeKok" books, however, that he is best known. *Every* year more than 700,000 Dutch people check a "Baantjer/DeKok" out of a library. The Dutch version of the Reader's Digest Condensed Books (called "Best Books" in Holland) has selected a Baantjer/DeKok book seven (7) times for inclusion in its series of condensed books.

Baantjer writes about Detective-Inspector DeKok of the Amsterdam Municipal Police (Homicide). Baantjer is himself a former inspector of the Amsterdam Police and is able to give his fictional characters the depth and the personality of real characters encountered during his long (38 years) police career. Many people in Holland sometimes confuse real-life Baantjer with fictional DeKok. The careful, authorized translations of his work published by InterContinental Publishing should fascinate the English speaking world as it has the Dutch reading public.

Murder in Amsterdam
Baantjer

The two very first "DeKok" stories for the first time in a single volume. In these stories DeKok meets Vledder, his invaluable assistant, for the first time. The book contains two complete novels. In *DeKok and the Sunday Strangler*, DeKok is recalled from his vacation in the provinces and tasked to find the murderer of a prostitute. The young, "scientific" detectives are stumped. Soon, a second corpse is found. At the last moment DeKok is able to prevent a third murder. In *DeKok and the Corpse on Christmas Eve*, a patrolling constable sees a floating corpse in a canal. Autopsy reveals that she has been strangled and that she was pregnant. "Silent witnesses" from the purse of the murdered girl point to two men. The fiancee is suspect, but who is the second man? In order to preserve his Christmas Holiday, DeKok wants to solve the case quickly.

ISBN 1 881164 00 4

The two novellas make an irresistible case for the popularity of the Dutch author. DeKok's maverick personality certainly makes him a compassionate judge of other outsiders and an astute analyst of antisocial behavior
    —*Marilyn Stasio*, **The New York Times Book Review**

This first translation of Baantjer's work into English supports the mystery writer's reputation in his native Holland as a Dutch Conan Doyle. His knowledge of esoterica rivals that of Holmes, but Baantjer wisely uses such trivia infrequently, his main interests clearly being detective work, characterization and moral complexity.   —**Publishers Weekly**

Both stories are very easy to take.   —**Kirkus Reviews**

DeKok and the Somber Nude
Baantjer

The oldest of the four men turned to DeKok: "You're from Homicide?" DeKok nodded. The man wiped the raindrops from his face, bent down and carefully lifted a corner of the canvas. Slowly the head became visible: a severed girl's head. DeKok felt the blood drain from his face. "Is that all you found?" he asked. "A little further," the man answered sadly, "is the rest." Spread out among the dirt and the refuse were the remaining parts of the body: both arms, the long, slender legs, the petite torso. There was no clothing.

First American edition of this European Best-Seller.

ISBN 1 881164 01 2

Baantjer's laconic, rapid-fire storytelling has spun out a surprisingly complex web of mysteries. —**Kirkus Reviews**

It's easy to understand the appeal of Amsterdam police detective DeKok. —*Charles Solomon*, **Los Angeles Times**

DeKok and Murder on the Menu
Baantjer

On the back of a menu from the Amsterdam Hotel-Restaurant *De Poort van Eden* (Eden's Gate) is found the complete, signed confession of a murder. The perpetrator confesses to the killing of a named blackmailer. Inspector DeKok (Amsterdam Municipal Police, Homicide) and his assistant, Vledder, gain possession of the menu. They remember the unsolved murder of a man whose corpse, with three bullet holes in the chest, was found floating in the waters of the Prince's Canal. A year-old case which was almost immediately turned over to the Narcotics Division. At the time it was considered to be just one more gang-related incident. DeKok and Vledder follow the trail of the menu and soon more victims are found and DeKok and Vledder are in deadly danger themselves. Although the murder was committed in Amsterdam, the case brings them to Rotterdam and other, well-known Dutch cities such as Edam and Maastricht.

First American edition of this European Best-Seller.

ISBN 1 881164 31 4

DeKok and the Sorrowing Tomcat
Baantjer

Peter Geffel (Cunning Pete) had to come to a bad end. Even his Mother thought so. Still young, he dies a violent death. Somewhere in the sand dunes that help protect the low lands of the Netherlands he is found by an early jogger, a dagger protruding from his back. The local police cannot find a clue. They inform other jurisdictions via the police telex. In the normal course of events, DeKok (Homicide) receives a copy of the notification. It is the start of a new adventure for DeKok and his inseparable side-kick, Vledder. Baantjer relates the events in his usual, laconic manner.

First American edition of this European Best-Seller.

ISBN 1 881164 05 5

The pages turn easily and DeKok's offbeat personality keeps readers interested. **—Publishers Weekly**

TENERIFE! by Elsinck

Madrid 1989. The body of a man is found in a derelict hotel room. The body is suspended, by means of chains, from hooks in the ceiling. A gag protrudes from the mouth. He has been tortured to death. Even hardened police officers turn away, nauseated. And this won't be the only murder. Quickly the reader becomes aware of the identity of the perpetrator, but the police are faced with a complete mystery. What are the motives? It looks like revenge, but what do the victims have in common? Why does the perpetrator prefer black leather cuffs, blindfolds and whips? The hunt for the assassin leads the police to seldom frequented places in Spain and Amsterdam, including the little known world of the S&M clubs in Amsterdam's Red Light District. In this spine-tingling thriller the reader follows the hunters, as well as the hunted and Elsinck succeeds in creating near unendurable suspense.

First American edition of this European Best-Seller.

ISBN 1 881164 51 9

A fascinating work combining suspense and the study of a troubled mind to tell a story that compels the reader to continue reading. **—Mac Rutherford, Lucky Books**

. . . A wonderful plot, well written — Strong first effort — Promising debut — A successful first effort. A find! — A well written book, holds promise for the future of this author — A first effort to make dreams come true — A jewel of a thriller! — An excellent book, gripping, suspenseful and extremely well written . . .
— A sampling of Dutch press reviews

MURDER BY FAX by Elsinck

Elsinck's second effort consists entirely of a series of Fax copies. An important businessman receives a fax from an organization calling itself "The Radical People's Front for Africa". It demands a contribution of $5 million to aid the struggle of the black population in South Africa. The reader follows the alleged motives and criminal goals of the so-called organization via a series of approximately 200 fax messages between various companies, police departments and other persons. All communication is by Fax and it will lead, eventually, to kidnapping and murder. Tension is maintained throughout and the reader experiences the vicarious thrill of "reading someone else's mail".

First American edition of this European Best-Seller.

ISBN 1 881164 52 7

Elsinck has created a technical tour-de-force: This high-tech version of the epistolary novel succeeds as the faxed messages quickly prove capable of providing plot, clues and characterization. **—Publishers Weekly**

This novel by Dutch author Elsinck is so interestingly written it might be read for its creative style alone. It is sharp and concise and one easily becomes involved enough to read it in one sitting. MURDER BY FAX cannot help but have its American readers fall under the spell of this highly original author.
—Paulette Kozick, West Coast Review of Books

This clever and breezy thriller is a fun exercise. The crafty Dutch author peppers his fictional fax copies with clues and red herrings that make you wonder who's behind the scheme. Elsinck's spirit of inventiveness keeps you guessing up to the satisfying end. **—Timothy Hunter, (Cleveland) Plain Dealer**

. . . Riveting—Sustains tension and is totally believable—An original idea, well executed—Unorthodox—Engrossing and frightening—Well conceived, written and executed—Elsinck sustains his reputation as a major new writer of thrillers . . .
—A sampling of Dutch press reviews

CONFESSION OF A HIRED KILLER

by Elsinck

A dead man is found in a small house on the remote Greek island of Serifos. His sole legacy consists of an incomplete letter, still in the typewriter. An intensive investigation reveals that the man may well be an independent, hired killer. His "clients" apparently included the Mafia and the Cosa Nostra. The trail leads from the Mediterranean to Berkeley, California and with quick scene changes and a riveting style, Elsinck succeeds again in creating a high tempo and sustained tension. A carefully documented thriller which exposes the merciless methods of organized crime. In 1990 Elsinck burst on the scene with the much talked-about *Tenerife!* which was followed, in 1991, with *Murder by Fax*. His latest offering has all the elements of another best-seller.

First American edition of this European Best-Seller.

ISBN 1 881164 53 5

Elsinck saves a nice surprise, despite its wild farrago of murder and assorted intrigue.   **— Kirkus Reviews**

. . . Elsinck remains a valuable asset to the thriller genre. He is original, writes in a lively style and researches his material with painstaking care . . .   **— de Volkskrant, Amsterdam**

What Others Say About Our Books
(a sampling of critical reviews provided by our readers)

About BAANTJER, the author of the "DeKok" books: The Reader's Digest has already used seven books by Baantjer in *Het Beste Boek* (Best Books), to great enjoyment of our readers (*L.C.P Rogmans*, Editor-in-Chief, [Dutch] Reader's Digest); A Baantjer book is checked out of a library more than 700,000 times per year (Netherlands Library Information Service); We have to put the second printing of his books on press before the first printing has even reached the bookstores, no matter how many we print (*Wim Hazeu*, Baantjer's Dutch Publisher).

About MURDER IN AMSTERDAM (ISBN 1-881164-00-4) by Baantjer: The two novellas make an irresistible case for the popularity of the Dutch author. DeKok's maverick personality certainly makes him a compassionate judge of other outsiders and an astute analyst of antisocial behavior (*Marilyn Stasio*, The New York Times Book Review); Both stories are very easy to take (Kirkus Reviews); This first translation of Baantjer's work into English supports the mystery writer's reputation in his native Holland as a Dutch Conan Doyle. His knowledge of esoterica rivals that of Holmes, but Baantjer wisely uses such trivia infrequently, his main interests clearly being detective work, characterization and moral complexity (Publishers Weekly).

About DEKOK AND THE SOMBER NUDE (ISBN 1-881164-01-2) by Baantjer: It's easy to understand the appeal of Amsterdam police detective DeKok (*Charles Solomon*, Los Angeles Times); Baantjer's laconic, rapid-fire storytelling has spun out a surprisingly complex web of mysteries (Kirkus Reviews).

About DEKOK AND THE DEAD HARLEQUIN (ISBN 1-881164-04-7) by Baantjer: Baantjer's latest mystery finds his hero in fine form. As in Baantjer's earlier works, the issue of moral ambiguity once again plays heavily as DeKok ultimately solves the crimes (Publishers Weekly).

About DEKOK AND THE SORROWING TOMCAT (ISBN 1-881164-05-5): The pages turn easily and DeKok's offbeat personality keeps readers interested. (Publishers Weekly).

About DEKOK AND MURDER ON THE MENU (ISBN 1-881164-31-4) by Baantjer: Nobody seems to have reviewed this (our first) book, but it is in its 11th (eleventh) printing (since 1990) in Holland.

What others say about ELSINCK:

About TENERIFE! (ISBN 1-881164-51-9) by Elsinck: A fascinating work combining suspense and the study of a troubled mind to tell a story that compels the reader to continue reading (*Mac Rutherford*, Lucky Books); . . . A wonderful plot, well written—Strong first effort—Promising debut—A successful first effort. A find!—A well written book, holds promise for the future of this author—A first effort to make dreams come true—A jewel of a thriller!—An excellent book, gripping, suspenseful and extremely well written . . . (A sampling of Dutch press reviews).

About MURDER BY FAX (ISBN 1-881164-52-7) by Elsinck: Elsinck has created a technical tour-de-force. This high-tech version of the epistolary novel succeeds as the faxed messages quickly prove capable of providing plot, clues and characterization (Publishers Weekly); This novel by Dutch author Elsinck is so interestingly written it might be read for its creative style alone. It is sharp and concise and one easily becomes involved enough to read it in one sitting. MURDER BY FAX cannot help but have its American readers fall under the spell of this highly original author (*Paulette Kozick*, West Coast Review of Books); This clever and breezy thriller is a fun exercise. The crafty Dutch author peppers his fictional fax copies with clues and red herrings that make you wonder who's behind the scheme. Elsinck's spirit of inventiveness keeps you guessing up to the satisfying end (*Timothy Hunter*, [Cleveland] Plain Dealer); The use of modern technology is nothing new, but Dutch writer Elsinck takes it one step further (*Peter Handel*, San Francisco Chronicle) . . . Riveting—Sustains tension and is totally believable—An original idea, well executed—Unorthodox—Engrossing and frightening—Well conceived, written and executed—Elsinck sustains his reputation as a major new writer of thrillers . . . (A sampling of Dutch press reviews).

About CONFESSION OF A HIRED KILLER (ISBN 1-881164-53-5) by Elsinck: Elsinck saves a nice surprise, despite its wild farrago of murder and assorted intrigue (Kirkus Reviews); Elsinck remains a valuable asset to the thriller genre. He is original, writes in a lively style and researches his material with painstaking care (de Volkskrant, Amsterdam).

INTERCONTINENTAL PUBLISHING does not have a clipping service. These reviews come to us by courtesy of our many fans and readers of quality mystery books.